A
THINKING
MAN'S
BULLY

A
THINKING
MAN'S
BULLY

**UNSTUCK IN TIME, UNBURDENED BY
CONVENTION, AND LIBERATED FROM FACT**

MICHAEL ADELBERG

THE PERMANENT PRESS
Sag Harbor, NY 11963

For information, address:
    The Permanent Press
    4170 Noyac Road
    Sag Harbor, NY 11963
    www.thepermanentpress.com

Library of Congress Cataloging-in-Publication Data

    Adelberg, Michael– .
        A thinking man's bully : unstuck in time, unburdened by
    convention, and liberated from fact / Michael Adelberg.
            p. cm.
        ISBN 978-1-57962-228-2
            1. Fathers and sons—Fiction. 2. Bullying—Fiction. I. Title.

    PS3601.D4666T48 2011
    813'.6—dc23   2011027190

Printed in the United States of America.

Dedication

This book is dedicated to
Eric Adelberg, 1990–2010,
an unbelievably cool nephew to
an unbelievably grumpy uncle, and
a great brother and son to his family.

We love you and miss you.

Acknowledgements

One night, a few years ago, I woke up at two-fifteen and started writing a novel. I had no experience writing fiction and knew the odds of success were slim. Fortunately, a small group of highly literate and decent people helped me again and again as I learned to write fiction the hard way—one miserable draft after another. Without them, my novel, *A Thinking Man's Bully*, never could have made it to print.

Joe Donohue, my childhood friend, hated the early drafts of the book and respected me enough to tell me so. Joe pushed me toward action-oriented narrative and his many suggestions melded a collection of stories into a novel.

Sally "Lady Red Pencil" Ketchum thought my early drafts were prolix or worse. The word count of her comments sometimes equaled the word count of the chapter she was reviewing. Under Sally's stern hand, sentences shrunk to eight words and dialogue sharpened.

Tom Miglino was the one-man fan club who kept me going. Tom found passages that moved him, and others that made him laugh. While he offered helpful criticisms, Tom was the essential good-cop whose kind words balanced the beatings from the bad-cops.

Judy Adelberg, my mother, read the manuscript end-to-end four times and each time provided meticulous comments on word choice, sentence construction, and flow. She was alternately a taskmaster or a cheerleader depending upon what I needed.

Bob Adams, Kate De Medeiros, Chris Green, Chris Koepke, and Mark Zobel also provided helpful feedback. Ted Sturtz's intrepid e-periodical, *The New York Journal of Books,* provided me with the forum for getting noticed. Marty and Judy Shepard gave a first-time novelist an open-minded examination and excellent feedback, a rarity in publishing these days.

Finally, I thank my wife, Joanne, for indulging all of my introversions. Writing this very personal novel was hard for me, and, at times, harder for her.

Contents

❧

Introduction

My best friend from high school blew his brains out at the end of our junior year. It was the day after I punched him in the face over something stupid. Other than his parents, I was the only person mentioned in his suicide note. That was twenty-three years ago. I never shed a tear.

A year ago, Jack, my fifteen-year-old son, attempted suicide. He would have completed the deed were it not for me finding him before all the blood ran out of his arms. The suicide note suggests that I was one of the reasons he decided to take his life. I never shed a tear.

These two awful events must say something about me.

Shortly after Jack's attempted suicide, I started seeing Lisa Moscovitz, a psychiatrist. This was at the earnest request of my wife, Diane. The therapy was not to help me deal with post-event depression or diminishment. I continued to perform well at work, sleep through the night, eat three 'squares' a day, move my bowels regularly, and raise an erection when called upon. Rather, the purpose of the therapy was to prove or disprove the hypothesis that there is something about me that moved two critically important people in my life toward suicide—and to identify, if the hypothesis is correct, the behaviors in me that have to be modified.

My first few sessions with Lisa were, by her judgment, "super-ficial and unhelpful" because I "did not bring my full self" into the conversations. Always shy when talking about myself, perhaps this was to be expected. Lisa confessed frustration after our third session and told me that she would end her one-year commitment to work with me if I was not more communicative. Knowing that I am a professional writer—a grant writer, not a real author—Lisa asked me if I could be more honest with her if I wrote down my memories and emailed them to her before each session. I agreed to give it a try.

Lisa's assignment for me was to look back, think hard, and write about the people and events that led to the death of my best friend and the near-suicide of my son. Each week for five months, I wrote about an incident or person that figured in the lead-up to one of these events. I found it easier to write honestly than to speak freely. I cannot bring back my dead friend, but *if* I can come clean, perhaps I can make myself into the father my son needs.

Therapeutics aside, recording these events released the author bottled up inside me. To my surprise, my oldest friends—Patrick McGowan, Kevin Kopf, Lynette Robson—and my persevering wife, Diane, loved the stories. At their collective urging, I now offer them to you in two sections: *The Book of McDuff* about my high school years and *The Book of Jack* about my son.

I begin, however, by recounting two recent conversations that needed to occur before this book could see print: a recent incident with my father that sheds light on why I am the person I have become, and a scab-pulling conversation with the parents of my dead old friend.

I LIVE at 24 Mayfair Way in East Princeton, New Jersey with my wife of eighteen years, Diane, and son, Jack. We have a small, three-bedroom house with a two-and-a-half-car garage. The garage is larger than our front or backyard. Despite its proximity to the village of Princeton and its famous university, virtually no Princeton

University professionals live in East Princeton. Many drive through it to live in deeper-rooted communities such as Hightstown and Cranbury. I think this is snobbery. East Princeton is a perfectly nice, newer New Jersey suburb. This is proven by the presence of our own Whole Foods supermarket—that great barometer of suburban desirability.

East Princeton is too far from either New York City or Philadelphia for easy daily commutes. Most homeowners drive to various office parks in central New Jersey. Others hold positions that suckle at the teat of state government in nearby Trenton. Everything good about New Jersey—the shore, access to NYC and Philly, the Six Flags amusement park, the Meadowlands sports arenas, the Delaware Water Gap—is sixty to ninety minutes away. But New Jerseyians accept that anything desirable requires a long drive. The only knock I have against East Princeton is that it is a borderland between the New York-leaning and Philadelphia-leaning parts of the state. So certain classless neighbors kill me every time the Eagles beat the Giants, the Phillies beat the Mets, the Sixers beat the Knicks, or the Flyers beat the Rangers—all sadly frequent occurrences in recent years.

East Princeton is about three-quarters native-born white, with an assortment of different-looking people sprinkled among us. This is perfect diversity to the modern white suburbanite—a few people from everywhere on the globe, but no group numerous enough to constitute a rival community. No one living in East Princeton is *from* East Princeton; twenty years ago, it was all farmland. The farm families that previously owned the land cashed out for big money in the early 1990s and now live as country squires in the Carolinas.

Three miles from my house is suite 21B of the Meadows Glenn professional building. This is the office of Lisa Moscovitz, my shrink. The hollow aluminum 'marble' columns on the building's exterior are surpassed in cheesiness only by the gas fireplace inside Lisa's office. At the entrance of her office suite is a small waiting room recently updated with 2008 issues of *Newsweek* and *Cosmo*. The coffee is even older. Lisa's office contains the requisite cherry-finished desk and leather couch. There's also an L.L.Bean rocking chair by the gas fireplace where I typically sit. East Princeton is the setting for *The Book of Jack* and the 'Discussions with Lisa' that occur throughout this book.

I was born and raised in Morganville, a half-hour east of East Princeton. It too was farmland until about 1970 when developers bought up the farms and chopped the land into half and quarter-acre residential lots. Morganville was, and still is, a good mailing address. I grew up in a subdivision called Battleview Acres, named in honor of a Revolutionary War battlefield that was paved over to create it.

When I attended Morganville High School in the mid-1980s, it was considered a good school with that key trait sought by the parents who moved their families from New York City to Morganville— a non-diverse student body. Over half of the school's graduates went straight into a four-year college. Morganville High School was so extraordinarily safe and non-diverse that my friends and I were correctly short-listed among the school's arch-nonconformists, and even considered dangerous by some.

However, the center of my teenage universe was not high school. It was Freedom Tree Park. This was a state-of-the-art recreational park built atop wetlands at the junction of Battleview Acres and the ritzy, newer subdivision of Excelsior Oaks. The park included four tennis courts, two basketball courts, skateboard ramps, a baseball field, a soccer field, and a roller hockey rink. Regardless of the season, most of the park's athletic amenities went fallow. Within five years, the athletic fields were filled with weeds and the over-shaded tennis courts fell into mossy disuse.

The park was named after the Freedom Tree, an oak long gone at the junction of two Revolutionary War-era roads from which pro-British Loyalists were hanged. A plaque in the park describes the Freedom Tree, complete with a bronzed sketch of a rotting corpse hanging from a tree limb and a smiling colonial family in the sketch's foreground. A year after the park's dedication, historians proved that the Freedom Tree plaque was placed there by convenience rather than historical accuracy. The true location of the actual Freedom Tree was a half-mile away, in the present-day parking lot of the local ShopRite.

Morganville, circa 1987, is the setting for *The Book of McDuff*.

———·——

ABOUT FORTY years ago, my father, James Duffy, and his wife, Marisol, left Brooklyn with their seven- and nine-year-old sons, with a third (me) on the way. They relocated to Morganville along with two thousand other middle-class families fleeing New York City. The decision to move was made entirely by James; Marisol never wanted to move to the place she called "the land of make-believe." Lacking neighbors who cared about her two passions— Latin music and beat poetry—Marisol went into a state of resigned melancholy that lasted until her death thirty-five years later. I never knew the exuberant woman of my older brothers' child-hood stories.

My father still lives in Morganville, in the house where I grew up. This book is not about Dad, but it must start with him.

~ The End of the Story ~

1

Modest People Should Be

*E*stranged is a strange word—broad in its application, precise in its implication. It is applicable when two people who were formerly close grow distant; it is applicable when two people have a wall of tension between them that makes easy interaction impossible; it is applicable when family members cannot speak comfortably with each other. By any of these applications, I am estranged from my father.

Unlike most fathers who brought their families to Morganville in the early '70s, raised them, and moved out when the youngest child married, Dad never left. He's been alone since my mother died four years ago. Most of his contemporaries are gone, replaced by a new generation of suburban males Dad calls "sister-men."

Dad's house is pockmarked with discolored spots on the forty-year-old siding. The interior of the house is shrinking. Mom's death was the last time that a newspaper or magazine was thrown away, and piles of them now line the hallways and fill the dining room.

When I last attempted to throw out one of the piles of news-papers, Dad growled, "Hey, college boy. Put that pile down or you'll be wearing orthopedic shirts." Dad is of that generation of men who use the term 'college boy' as a grave put down. I tell myself that Dad is secretly proud that all three of his boys went to college and made it into white collar jobs, but since he's never said so, I know this may be wishful thinking.

Dad's either seventy-six or seventy-seven. He is a big man: six feet three and 225 pounds, resembling a bald Clint Eastwood. But he shrinks when he leans forward and squints. I had to calm him down three weeks ago when he believed the CVS cashier shorted him four dollars. He called the poor West Indian cashier "a crook and a liar." I took a five-dollar bill out of my wallet, put it in his hand, and said, "Dad, here. You're now up a dollar. Let's get out of here before they ban you from the store."

Dad confuses names and shows no ability to remember the name of my wife, Diane. Recently, he shouted to her across a restaurant, "Hey, Roxanne or Joanne or whatever, can you get me a beer from the bar? The waitress is never going to get here." Dad's never liked Diane; I wonder if his inability to recall her name is an extended joke.

To his credit, Dad avoids nostalgia. He complains, "The good old days sucked." Perhaps this comes from his career: until he was thirty-seven, Dad was a New York City cop; then he nearly killed himself saving a Chinese immigrant from a burning sweatshop. For this, he received a medal from Mayor Lindsay and a little picture of himself in the *Daily News*. After the near-death experience, Dad left the NYPD. He went for the money, taking a job running theft-prevention for Jamesway—a New Jersey department store chain—and moved his family to New Jersey. He hated this job, but his mortgage and family of five made it impossible to go back to police work. Dad spent the rest of his work life miserable, running "loss recovery" programs for different New Jersey retailers. He spent the next twenty-five years outwitting crooks, but not clever or dangerous ones—just dumbass teenagers stuffing CDs into their coats and cigarettes into their jeans.

———

MOST MORNINGS, Dad wakes up at five-thirty and sends off three or four blistering emails to his Congressman or his sons before finishing his coffee. He watches "that socialist Matt Lauer" on *The*

Today Show as his primary source of news. By seven, he's eaten his standard breakfast—three scrambled eggs and whole wheat toast—and begun his day.

He drives to the senior center in Freehold, plays bridge for a couple of hours, goes to CVS or the supermarket, and heads home by one PM to send a few more blistering emails about whatever outrages he learned of at the senior center that morning. Because my brothers both live out of state and do what they can to avoid dealing with Dad, I draw sole responsibility for handling his frequent pseudo-emergencies.

The most recent pseudo-emergency came a week ago in the Morganville ShopRite parking lot. Dad was driving closely behind a gold Infiniti sedan. The car had a bumper sticker that read "Modest People Should Be!" and listed a 1-800 number for some self-help program that teaches people to seize life by the pubic hairs and make it cry uncle. For thirty years Dad's shouted "Modest People Should Be!" to counter people scolding him for his immodest statements. He claims to have invented the phrase, and I believe him.

At ShopRite that morning, Dad tailgated the Infiniti as he squinted and leaned forward to read the bumper sticker of the EST[1] knockoff that had stolen his catchphrase. When the sedan stopped at a speed bump, Dad ran his '97 Taurus wagon into the sedan's rear. The accident occurred at ten MPH, so no one was seriously hurt. But Dad received a bruise on his forehead that left him looking like Mikhail Gorbachev.

Dad called me at work and matter-of-factly stated, "I scratched the bumper of another car. I need you to deal with the hysterical Jew who owns it. I think she's about to call in the Israeli military for air strikes. Matt, I can't take all of this drama."

He then put the woman on the phone. Two hours later, the crisis was averted: the estimate from the Infiniti dealer was $1,800 for a new bumper and rear lights. I wrote the driver a check and delivered it to her house in exchange for her not reporting the

---

1. EST was a prolific pop-psychology business in the 1980s and '90s.

incident to the insurance company. This had the practical effect of keeping Dad's insurance rates artificially low, and delaying the day when I will have to pry the car keys out of his clenched fist.

Dad's never once thanked me for the time I devote to bailing him out of his problems. But as I drove him home that day, he surprised me by asking, "How's your book coming?" I told Dad about the book two weeks earlier and figured—given his faltering memory and sparse communications—that he would never ask about it.

I proudly said, "I'm doing a check of the editor's proof now. It should go to print in a few weeks."

"Well, my son's an author. Even though it's a nutcase book, I guess this proves I did something right raising you." The line was quintessentially Dad. I did something great without a stitch of help from him, and he both minimized the accomplishment and took credit for it at the same time. I didn't say anything, but started thinking about my next book: a fictional memoir in which a no-good son kills his parents to speed up his inheritance, gets caught, and writes his remorseless confession from death row.

As we pulled into Dad's driveway, he said, "You know, Matt, you need to talk with the Rosens about your book before it gets printed."

I said, "I know, Dad." But up to that point, the thought had not crossed my mind.

2

Diamond Smiles

Last Saturday morning, I rang the doorbell of the Rosens' house. Mrs. Rosen called "Who's there?" as she started opening the door.

I said, "It's Matt Duffy, Mrs. Rosen, hope you remember me." But the sound of the bottom of the door rubbing on the high carpeting drowned out my voice.

She stared at me for a few seconds—studying my face. Then her eyes widened and she smiled. "Oh, my God! Matthew Duffy! It's so good to see you. What's it been—almost twenty years? It's chilly outside, please come in."

Thirty-five years away from New York and Mrs. Rosen still had a slight New York City accent. Her hair was dyed L'Oréal orange, that unnatural shade chosen only by aging women. Two vertical skin folds hung underneath her chin. I saw them wobble as she leaned forward to open the door. I hated myself for thinking that Mrs. Rosen looked like a turkey.

I was relieved that she was happy to see me; I was worried that the door might slam in my face. Mrs. Rosen gave me a hug as I came into the house. My hands were full, so I just stood there as she squeezed me. She called upstairs, "Arn, come down. We have a very special visitor."

I followed Mrs. Rosen into the living room. Nearly everything in the room had changed in the two decades since I was last in it, but I did see two touchstones. First, there was still the same rickety sliding door to the backyard. I remembered the many times I snuck in and out of the Rosen house, worrying that the metallic squeak of that door would be my doom. Then I saw that same glass candy bowl on the coffee table. I remembered that bowl stuffed with marijuana—and flushing it down the toilet—and scooping the licorice candies back in the bowl just as Mr. and Mrs. Rosen returned home. I remembered concealing my laughter as Mr. Rosen saw me, and said, "Oh, hi Matt. You must really like licorice." It looked like the same licorice candies were still in the bowl.

I was carrying a box of stuff that originally belonged to the Rosen's middle child. Though it wasn't very heavy, my arm ached from carrying the bulky box up the street from Dad's house. My other arm was encumbered too, carrying a loose-leaf binder containing my book manuscript. I set both at the foot of an easy chair where I sat down, and shook my arms to get the blood flowing again.

Mr. Rosen entered the room. He was hunched over slightly, and I noticed a hearing aid in one of his ears. He wore awful-looking sneakers, the cheap kind sold at Target. But besides this, I was impressed with how good he looked—clean-shaven and fit. I hated that he had more hair on his head than me.

Mr. Rosen gave me a firm handshake and a hard pat on the shoulder. "Well, Matthew 'McDuff' Duffy. What the hell ya doin' calling on a couple of old fogies like us?"

Before I could answer, Mrs. Rosen interjected, "Old fogies my eye. Arn, you're so rude." Then she turned to me, "Tell us about your lovely wife and child."

The Rosens settled on the couch a few feet from me and both leaned forward. I only ask about people's families to fill dead air during awkward social exchanges, but they looked genuinely interested.

I cleared my throat and started. "Well, all is fine with the family. Jack's a high school sophomore this year. Like his father at that age, he's not much of a student. But he wrestled varsity this year and has a brown belt in karate. He's a wonderful athlete and very witty. A lot of girls call for him." I then thought about Jack's problems: his under-performance in school, his bullying, and the terrible scars on his wrists from his attempted suicide.

I decided not to mention any of this and pushed forward, "Diane is doing fine too. She's working again—teaching kindergarten at a small private school in Flemington. She keeps me in line, her real full-time job." Having offered the requisite quick report on my family, I said, "So, tell me about the Rosen clan."

Mr. Rosen opened his mouth to speak but Mrs. Rosen went first, "Oh, Rachel and Joseph are doing just great in Atlanta. The grandkids—Amy and William—are such a, such a joy." She handed me a recent portrait of the family of their youngest child, Rachel, and her Ken-doll physician husband. Without pausing she continued, "Warren is still living the life of the bachelor scholar. He's back from a year in China, and has written a book about his interviews with different Chinese factory owners." She handed me a book, *Scientific Management's Chinese Disciples.*

Mr. Rosen jumped in, "Warren says the Chinese are crazy about getting the most out of their workers, and they all read these century-old scientific management studies performed by an old American professor, Frederick Taylor. Warren's research proves . . ."

Mrs. Rosen took back the conversation again. "Warren's been back in Evanston for six months now with his housemate, John, teaching again at Northwestern." I was handed a picture of their oldest son, Warren, in full academic garb. My mind wandered as I remembered the esteemed Professor Rosen as a twenty-two-year-old Dead Head whose principal scholarly pursuit was cataloging the subtly different highs offered by different strains of marijuana.

Married for over forty years, Mr. Rosen understood the meaning of his wife's interruptions. He dutifully returned to family, "So that's a little about Rachel and Warren. As for Martin, there's not much to say. We thank you for being such a good friend to him." I looked across to see Mrs. Rosen's eyes tear up at the mention of their middle child.

I felt some guilt, but since Mr. Rosen had mentioned Martin, I had to begin. "Well, I want to talk with you both about Martin." I bent over to grab the loose-leaf binder at my feet. As I handed it to Mrs. Rosen, I continued. "I want you both to know that I have written a book about my junior year of high school and the way it impacted me as a parent."

Mrs. Rosen's eyes widened enthusiastically, Mr. Rosen's eyes narrowed skeptically.

"A publisher has agreed to publish it. I'm real excited." I paused briefly, thinking about the best words for my next sentence.

Mr. Rosen filled the silence, "But some *things* are in there about Martin."

"Yes, a lot." I answered.

There were a few seconds of silence. Mrs. Rosen started turning the pages of the manuscript, but too quickly to read anything. Mr. Rosen slouched into the couch, exhaled, and asked, "I'll bet your book is rough, isn't it?"

I nodded yes. "But Martin's not the only one who gets roughed up."

I changed the subject, sort of, by picking up the box of bric-a-brac and putting it at their feet. "These are the things I took out of Martin's room. I want to return them."

Mr. Rosen stuck a hand into the box of CDs, VHS tapes, and hockey paraphernalia. He emerged with a CD, *The Fine Art of Surfacing*, by the Boomtown Rats. "I remember this one. Martin played it all the time. The hit song was 'I Don't Like Mondays.' There's some nice piano in that song. I never knew it was about a teen killer until years later."

I nodded yes, but added, "Of course, you remember that Martin's favorite song on that album was 'Diamond Smiles.'" Seeing blank faces at this comment, I offered an explanation. "It's a sad song about a teenage girl who grows impatient with her shallow peers, so she chooses to," I stammered for the right words, "umm, take leave of them."

Mr. Rosen reddened; Mrs. Rosen looked down.

I stopped there. Silence followed.

Mrs. Rosen continued skimming the pages of my manuscript. She stopped on a page in the middle of the loose-leaf and started reading it. She smiled—the bright lipstick on her lips exaggerated her smile. I remembered Martin telling me that his mother looked like the Joker—the Batman villain—when she smiled. It was true. Then I heard her grunt. The smile was gone. I craned my neck to see where she was in the book, but the top of the binder blocked my view.

There was more silence. Finally, I said, "I wanted you to know about the book and have a chance to read it before it goes to print." Mrs. Rosen smiled a little, but it did not conceal the tears in her eyes; now Mr. Rosen's eyes were also wet. He exhaled again.

More silence. They looked at each other, Mrs. Rosen nodded to her husband. He understood.

Mr. Rosen stood up, and motioned for me to rise. As I stood, I said, "I would like to leave the box and the manuscript with you."

Mrs. Rosen stood as well. She leaned over, and gave me a peck on the cheek. I leaned in to hug her, but she had already withdrawn.

Mr. Rosen took my arm and led me toward the front door. He made small talk by complaining about his house of thirty-five years. "It's getting too big for us." he said, "We'll be downsizing in a year or two."

I felt a need to say something, but he kept speaking without providing the necessary pause. As he opened the door, Mr. Rosen's voice and posture became formal. He said, "Matthew, thank you for stopping by and letting us see your book. We will read it."

I stepped out of the house and turned around to say goodbye, but the door was already closed.

As I walked down the street toward Dad's house, I passed the split-level that used to belong to the Flannery's. I looked up the driveway to the spot where I humiliated myself while humiliating my childhood playmate, Bobby Flannery. I shook my head.

~ THE BOOK OF MCDUFF ~

3

Mr. Salty

M r. Salty was the mascot for a local pretzel brand of the same name—a stick figure made of pretzel rods. Due to his brittle dough body and high salt content, Mr. Salty suffered from chronic joint stiffness and hypertension. Despite this, he was optimistic and kind, but maybe just a little bit simpleminded. Each night, while standing vertically in the pretzel bag with his twenty brothers and sisters, Mr. Salty prayed to the great God of Snack Foods that one day he would become a human boy. Then on a brilliant spring morning, in the only miracle I ever witnessed, Mr. Salty was magically transformed, like Pinocchio, into a young man. He became Bobby Flannery, the oldest child in the nice family that lived next door to mine. Or so went the legend of Mr. Salty, as constantly retold by me to every boy in Battleview Acres.

The real life story of Bobby Flannery was a little different. Though I never would have admitted it twenty years ago, Bobby Flannery was not really born as a collection of pretzel rods. He was, however, optimistic and kind, but maybe just a little bit simpleminded. Bobby was the only son and oldest child in the Flannery family. It is also true that his boney body and Gumby-walk made him the closest human equivalent to Mr. Salty anyone this side of the great God of Snack Foods was ever likely to see.

Bobby was five years older than my friends and me. Despite this, he was like a peer—and a rather submissive one at that. Due to his physical impairment, I never gave Bobby a bad time for avoiding after-school hockey. Although I was already a lapsed Catholic by age sixteen, I understood that there was nothing slimier than picking on someone for a physical disability. However, taking advantage of Bobby's less visible shortcomings was fair game.

———•———

By junior year of high school, I had pretty much lost interest in board games. But there were still a few times a year—usually holidays when my parents exerted what was left of their waning influence—when the Monopoly and Risk games still came out. When they did, I spent some 'wholesome time' being conquered financially or militarily. Bobby and the Dog—the boy who lived three houses past the Flannerys'—always participated in these games. The Dog never admitted liking what he termed "bored games," but when invited, he'd be at my door in five minutes. Whether it was just the three of us or there were more players, games generally followed the same plot:

- ♦ Act I—the Dog and I cajole Bobby into unfavorable deals or treaties
- ♦ Act II—Bobby is reduced to near-nothing, and through acts of meager charity, we keep him around
- ♦ Act III—the Dog wipes out Bobby before taking out other opponents

However, there was one game of Risk that deviated from this script. We began the game by dealing the cards to assign countries to each player. By a stroke of remarkable good luck, Bobby was dealt the entire continent of North America. Bobby started rocking back and forth and even trash-talking a little—in his own G-rated way—repeating, "I am going to beat your butts this time."

The first few turns, I retreated out of Australia and Asia, allowing the Dog to take them. This gave the Dog nine bonus armies a turn, enough to restore the natural order. But Bobby, having already collected extra armies for North America, swept me out of South America, countering the Dog's emergence on the Pacific Rim. I was reduced to a few low-rent spots in Europe and Africa.

A few turns later, the battle lines hardened and two massive armies stood across from each other on opposite sides of the Bering Strait. The Dog showed three Risk cards and quickly placed them at the bottom of the deck, allowing him to 'cash in' for extra troops. The quickness of the move alerted me that the Dog was probably cheating, but Bobby watched passively as the Dog plunked down twenty extra armies on Kamchatka. The Dog then launched his mighty attack against Bobby's forces in Alaska. Despite being slightly outnumbered, the luck of the dice was with Bobby, and the Dog's superiority sunk to parity as both armies took losses. After a few more bad rolls for the Dog, Bobby had the upper hand.

I started scat-singing the theme song from M*A*S*H, and helicoptered several of my armies to north Asia as reinforcements for the Dog. Bobby protested a bit—whining "Hey, McDuff, you can't do that." But considering the many basic rules of the game I was breaking—i.e., the rule forbidding two different players from merging armies, the rule against transferring armies to nonadjacent territories, and the rule against acting out of turn—Bobby's protests were meek and short in duration.

As Bobby acquiesced, the Dog noted, "History is filled with examples of small powers, like McDuff's mercenaries from northern Europe, tipping the balance in the wars of the great powers [the Dog and Bobby]. You may recall the decisive assistance of tiny Saxony, siding with England against France in the War of the Austrian Succession."

I am pretty sure this was total bullshit. The Dog often drew upon an imagined history of seventeenth- and eighteenth-century Europe to make a point. Just inserting 'Saxony' or 'Hesse-Cassel' into a sentence was enough for him to be perceived as authoritative. I have tried this once or twice since; it really works.

True to the Dog's concocted history, the ten extra troops I helicoptered to Kamchatka proved decisive and the Dog broke Bobby's defenses in Alaska. On the next turn, the Dog's reinforced armies poured into the thinly protected North American interior. (In so doing, this game of Risk validates Sarah Palin's warnings of the grave dangers faced by Alaskans as the sole line of defense against the bloodthirsty Yakuts of northern Asia.)

Other than his momentary protest a few turns earlier, Bobby demonstrated good sportsmanship as his remaining armies were eliminated from the Northwest Territories, British Columbia, Alberta, Ontario, Quebec, the eastern and western United States, Central America, and finally South America. The Dog completely wiped out Bobby before turning on my minimal forces—allowing me to claim second place.

Bobby's professional and romantic lives were as hapless as his life as a military commander. I know he attended one of those technical schools that advertised during *The People's Court*, but no job ever came from it. Dates were infrequent, and only when arranged by his older cousins.

He had a succession of low-end jobs: short-order cook at Denny's, security guard at an industrial park, customer service guy at a call center. During the gaps between jobs, he'd watch a ton of TV and make a little money selling lame products door-to-door, including frozen meat plans and vacuum cleaners. For the latter he memorized an oh-so-stale sales pitch from the 1960s, which included tossing a ball of manufacturer-supplied dirt into the middle of a carpeted floor and sucking it up. But Bobby quickly ran out of the ready-made dirt bombs, so he'd ask neighbors: "Please pretend there is a dirt bomb in my hand and that I'm tossing it onto your carpet." He then demonstrated the "amazing cleaning power" of his vacuum by vacuuming the already clean carpet. Sticking to the script, he'd ask his prospective customers, "Can you find even a single speck of dirt remaining?"

My parents always bought something from Bobby—inevitably the cheapest item he was selling. Dad reliably complained after each purchase about "the crap-tax" the Flannerys are putting on the families of Battleview Acres "to support their dim-wit son."

Toward the end of my junior year, Bobby started selling furniture and was successful enough to buy his own car. It was only a used Plymouth Reliant, but it was still a big step up from being driven to work by his mom. Time passed and I saw much less of him; when I did, he was usually with a girl going in or out of the Flannery house.

While walking to a hockey game at Freedom Tree Park one Saturday afternoon, the Dog and I saw Bobby and a girl leaving the Flannery house. She was carrying a milk crate containing some cleaning solutions; he was carrying a vacuum cleaner. I was curious.

I dropped my hockey bag, and called out "Yo, Salty." I jogged over to the two of them as they were loading Bobby's car. The Dog trailed a little behind.

Bobby gave me an awkward wave, turned away, and tried to look like he was carefully arranging the milk crate in the backseat of his car. As I approached I asked him, "Aren't you going to introduce me to your little friend?"

He stammered, "Uh, ya, McDuff, um, Matt Duffy, this is Rebecca." I shook hands with her. Besides wide hips, she was a good-looking girl. I remember thinking that she was way too pretty for someone like Bobby.

Tuning back to Bobby, I asked, "Where you going with the vacuum?"

Bobby straightened up and smiled, "I just rented an attic apartment in Freehold. It's a little dusty, so Rebecca and I are going over to clean it before I move in tomorrow."

To this day, I remember my exact reply, "Whew, for a minute I thought you were selling door to door again. My parents still complain about the last raft-load of shit they were guilted into buying from you."

There was no laughter. The four of us—Bobby, Rebecca, the Dog, and I—were silent for a while. Finally, the Dog said, "Wow! There's no happy after that one. We gotta go, *Bobby*. Hockey practice has already started." It was the first time in years that the Dog had called Bobby anything other than Mr. Salty—or Salty for short.

As we walked back to pick up our hockey bags, the Dog leaned into my ear and whispered, "You're an asshole." I didn't argue the point.

I looked back; Rebecca was giving Bobby a kiss on the cheek.

⸺•⸺

Mom and Pop Flannery are a few years older than my parents. Five years ago they sold their house and moved into a retirement community in southern New Jersey. Next-door neighbors for more than thirty years, my parents felt obligated to throw them a little party before they left Morganville. I didn't want to go, but Dad politely requested my attendance: "You better damn well be there. You grew up with these people. What's wrong with you?"

I saw middle-aged Bobby for the first time. His skinny frame is now accented by a small potbelly that protrudes like a swallowed volleyball. He wears thick glasses and most of his hair is gone. Bobby's Gumby-walk is more pronounced than ever—he steps from invisible bucket to invisible bucket as he moves—and his stammer is now a full-fledged stutter. Despite all of this, he's doing great.

Bobby married Rebecca close to twenty years ago. They have no children (medical tests proved that Bobby was sterile), but Bobby and Rebecca lovingly play the role of aunt and uncle to the two young children of Bobby's kid sister, Erin, and host an exchange student each year. Throughout the evening, I saw Bobby and Rebecca holding hands and making cow-eyes at each other. For the party's climax, my parents dimmed the living room lights, and Mrs. Miers—the neighborhood ham—narrated a slideshow about the Flannery family. In the shadows, Bobby and Rebecca smooched like teenagers.

I avoided Bobby and Rebecca all night. As people started leaving, Dad handed me two coats and said, "Hey, quit holding up the wall and bring these to Bobby Flannery and his wife."

I took the coats and walked across the room. "Hello Bobby, long time."

Bobby smiled, "Hi, um, Mc-McDuff. It's nice of your folks to do-do-do this for my pa-pa-parents, so many of the old fa-families are here. How's the Dog's fa-fa-family, I didn't see them to-tonight?"

"I don't really know. I haven't kept in touch with them."

Out of a sense of propriety, Bobby reintroduced me to Rebecca: "Oh, uh, Rebecca. This is McDuff. We g-g-grew up together."

I asked Rebecca, "Do you remember me?"

"Oh yes." She took her coat and exited the house.

Discussion with Lisa:

I entered Lisa's office. She motioned me to the leather couch opposite her desk. I passed the couch, and sat in the rocking chair that faced slightly away from her. I noisily unrolled the rubber band from the rolled-up copy of the story that I emailed her two days earlier, and started rocking.

"Matthew. Thanks for writing this story. It is good to finally hear your voice."

There was a pause. I knew she wanted me to do something. So I started reading "Mr. Salty" aloud.

Lisa sputtered, "Ah . . . um . . . uh. Matthew, I was speaking figuratively about your voice."

I stopped reading. Lisa looked at me, stone-faced. I tried to figure out what she was thinking.

"Do you believe it's true that introverts reveal themselves more on the page than through conversation?"

I nodded. We stared at each other some more.

Lisa started again, "Does this story help you see yourself as a bad kid who came to understand his mistakes, and therefore became a good adult?"

"Good as most." I said, not understanding my own answer.

This was going no better than our previous sessions.

I looked at her slightly masculine face—her stupid haircut with a curl at her shoulders. I thought about how she vaguely resembled George Washington. I transposed her face onto Mt. Rushmore and concluded that she was a dead ringer for GW. Her overly formal voice only reinforced that I was speaking with a statue, certainly something other than a real person. I thought about the time and money I was wasting.

"Did your friend, the Dog, really say those things about the War of the Austrian Succession?"

I looked up, happy to finally have a factual question I could answer, "Yes, and what's more amazing is that there's no evidence that he ever read anything other than the New York *Daily News* sports pages. He just seemed to know facts. He could name the entire cast of *Green Acres* or *Hogan's Heroes*, name the top goal scorer for every NHL team, or name every Frank Zappa album in chronological order. He knew everything about world history without ever reading a history book. He had an ability to string facts together with plausible faux facts to create convincing fake history, always perfectly customized for whatever point he was making."

My complete answer caught Lisa by surprise. I heard her whisper "unbelievable" under her breath.

I wondered, "Is she talking about the Dog or me?" Either way, I felt insulted.

"Have you ever apologized to Bobby Flannery?"

I became angry. "I bet you'd like me to chase down Bobby and offer him a heartfelt apology. In therapist circles, you'd boast about the repentant bully so completely in touch with himself that he's tracking down the children he wronged twenty years ago. You'd go to Geneva and present a paper about it. Maybe, you'd get a little Siggie award. No, the whole thing is a little too *My Name is Earl*." I laughed, "Peeling back scabs is difficult for everyone. No one wants to be reminded about their childhood humiliations. An apology from me to Bobby, however sincere, wouldn't help anyone."

"Peeling the scab would be hard for you, but why would it be hard for Bobby?"

I was adamant, "Tracking down Bobby and having a 'heart to heart' conversation is something a man just can't do."

"Please define 'a man' as you are using the word."

"Well, a man doesn't sit in an L.L.Bean rocking chair in a shrink's office easily discussing his guilt-filled moments."

"Why is the first story you wrote about a boy you treated so terribly?"

I smiled, "You didn't know me as a teen, I treated everyone like this. I had no choice but to write about a boy I treated terribly."

She cracked a smile, but only for a split second. "Do you always use humor as a mechanism to deflect serious questions? Before, I asked you to define a man, and you gave me an evasive response. Try again."

"Fine, I define a man as someone who uses humor as a mechanism for deflecting serious questions. Violence can be substituted for humor if necessary." For all of my attempts to stay hidden, Lisa had drawn me out. It was the first time I acknowledged that she was not a complete nitwit.

As I left Lisa's office, I started thinking about my next story. There were boys who suffered uglier bullying than anything inflicted upon Bobby Flannery. One of these boys would come next.

4

Hockey Rocky

With brand new CCM skates, an authentic Philadelphia Flyers jersey that formerly belonged to Ken "The Rat" Linseman (or so alleged), and bulging chest and shoulder muscles, Rocco D'Alessio was a sight to behold in or out of the roller hockey rink A rough stretch of puberty and the likely consumption of steroids littered Rocco's neck and shoulders with a combination of active acne volcanoes and craters from past ones. Acne aside, his long head and big front teeth gave him a face that even a mother could hate. And hate him we did: first, because he was a Flyers fan in a neighborhood of Rangers fans; second, because he was the only one in the neighborhood with new skates and hockey equipment; and third, because he was the only boy in Battleview Acres who played serious organized ice hockey—in hoity-toity Moorestown no less. So he was a lot better than us.

The D'Alessios moved in from the Philly 'burbs at the start of junior year and we took shots at Rocco from day one. On the roller hockey rink at Freedom Tree Park, he was clearly the best player: fastest skater, smoothest moves, and best slap-shot. Though never explicitly declared, a 'kill Rocco' parallel code of rules emerged to keep him in check. It was legal to hold, hook, and elbow Rocco. The abuse wrecked his confidence and had him icing the ball in preference to running the gauntlet of dirty back-checkers.

Unsure about the increasingly organized abuse, Rocco took the worst possible course of action by being a pussy. After a particularly vicious elbow from Kevin Kopf knocked Rocco backward on his ass, he stood up and laughed, "Well, I wasn't expectin' that," as if to say, "It's so funny that you're kicking my ass."

After that, dirty plays on Rocco were punctuated with mocking versions of that phrase. For example, I once tripped him into a face-first dive and asked, "Hey dick, were you expectin' that?" For all the laughter it induced, I felt terrible for days afterward. But I reminded myself that we all took shots at Rocco; it was not my fault if he wasn't sticking up for himself.

Then one November morning it happened: that defining incident in male circles that pushes a boy from the "guy *inside* the group that everyone picks on" to the "guy *outside* the group that everyone picks on." That morning I heard the theme song to *Rocky* coming through the garage door of the D'Alessio house. I heard grunts of "huhh . . . huhh" from Rocco from inside the garage, in addition to exhortations from his older brother: "Pump it up" and "one more rep and you'll be huge."

I ran back to my house and made some calls. Within fifteen minutes, four of us—the Dog, Patrick McGowan, Kevin Kopf, and I—were outside the D'Alessio garage. The D'Alessio boys by now had moved from the bench press to the heavy bag. The grunts of "huhh . . . huhh" continued interspersed with taunts to an imaginary Apollo Creed—no doubt reincarnated as the heavy bag. The witty repartee included such memorable lines as, "Got you now, Apollo Creed—huhh . . . huhh" and "This one's for the Italian Stallion—huhh."

After this, meetings with Rocco—now dubbed Hockey Rocky—became over-the-top mean. A chance encounter at the 7-Eleven included a chorus of "huhh" grunts and mock struggles as we lifted our Big Gulp sodas toward our mouths, and shoves when Rocco tried to get past us.

A conversation between Rocco and a girl in school he was known to like was broken up by Stallone-inflected calls of "Adrian! Adrian!" When ignored, our calls coarsened into shouts about Rocco's low I.Q. ("Yo Rock, you are dumber than a rock!") and worsening acne ("Rock, who dumped that sack of zits on top of you?"). Finally, a particularly vicious Kevin Kopf elbow landed square on Rocco's cheekbone at an after-school hockey game, sending Rocco home with a welt that took two weeks to fully disappear.

We saw little of Hockey Rocky after that. He stopped playing hockey with us and transferred to the Catholic high school, St. Joe's, midyear. I still saw Rocco every so often, usually jumping into or getting out of the car in his driveway. Even from afar, two things were inescapable—his expanding upper body and his worsening acne. The few times we made eye contact, he turned his glance away.

That spring, in the Freedom Tree Park roller hockey league, our gritty but under-skilled team started 0–3. I thought about Rocky's missing offense every time we lost a game, but never mentioned his name.

PATRICK McGOWAN also attended St. Joe's. One April night he took the Dog and me to a party in Old Bridge. The party was overcrowded with St. Joe's jocks and most of my friends left within an hour—after busting up the lawn furniture. This left just McGowan, the Dog, and me. The Dog stole a bottle of red wine and a bottle of green melon-flavored liquor from the host's parents' liquor cabinet. We passed around the bottles, drinking them in the host's garage. McGowan, the Dog, and I stumbled out a half-hour later—roaring drunk.

On our way to McGowan's car, I bumped heavily into the big chest and varsity jacket of some dumbass St. Joe's jock. I looked up. It was Hockey Rocky. We made eye contact, I said something like, "Pardon me, Mr. Mandarich"—a reference to the famously muscular, steroid-eating college football lineman who laid an egg in the NFL.

The dumbass didn't understand, but when one of his new friends explained the insult, Rocco called out, "Screw you, McDuff. I could bench press you and your whole family."

Even drunk, McGowan, the Dog, and I knew we had just heard one of the most mock-baiting lines in world history. So we walked back up the driveway toward Hockey Rocky performing a series of exaggerated bodybuilding poses. The Dog started blowing into his thumb, and on each breath puffed out his chest. McGowan started mouthing the theme music to *Rocky*, and the Dog and I both started on quotes from Hockey Rocky's garage. While no one besides Hockey Rocky knew exactly what we were doing, there was still a lot of laughter. One of his new friends, called out, "Rocco, they're making you look like a giant douchebag, and you're just standing there."

Dutifully, Rocco looked at me and said, "Shut your mouth or I'll shut it."

I said, "Thank you, Hockey Rocky, for that brilliant oration." Everyone laughed. Rocco came after me, but so slowly that it was easy for the wide-bodied McGowan and a dozen nameless jocks to get in between us.

As McGowan escorted me to his car, I heard the Dog taunt Hockey Rocky about how I would kick his ass. He appropriated lines from *Rocky* movies, shouting in the scratchy voice of Rocky's mentor, Mickey (Burgess Meredith), "He's a wrecking machine, Rock," and then the clincher, "He'll knock you into tomorrow, Rock." We laughed the entire ride home.

———

THE NEXT time I crossed paths with Hockey Rocky was a month later at a hockey game at Freedom Tree Park on the last weekend before the end of junior year. My team was wrapping up the season against a powerhouse team of ice hockey players from Old Bridge—with Hockey Rocky at right wing. The Dog, more or less the team captain, always asked me to neutralize the best scorer on the other team. The Old Bridge team had several gifted forwards, but when the Dog called across the rink, "McDuff, you cover that zit from Philadelphia," everyone knew my assignment.

Watching Rocky's shots during warm-ups, I knew his skills were sharper than ever. Looking at his huge chest, I whispered to McGowan, "With some green paint, he could be the Incredible Hulk."

Since Hockey Rocky started the game, I did too. On the first rush down toward my team's goal, I put my arm up the back of his jersey and forced him to drag me down the rink. As we went into the corner for a loose ball, I stepped hard on the blade of his stick and cracked it, forcing him to drop the stick and go back to the bench for a new one. I hid both moves from the ref and was treated to a hero's welcome as I returned to the bench.

The next time out, Hockey Rocky took a run at me, but I saw him coming and he made only glancing contact. He landed awkwardly on the boards and took himself out of the play. My team was rapturous, and started chanting "Rocky sucks!" The Dog shouted above everyone, in his Burgess Meredith voice, "You're a tomato can, Rock" and "He's gonna knock you into tomorrow, Rock."

Before this second shift was over, Hockey Rocky attempted to elbow me, but I ducked the worst of it and jabbed him in the chest with the butt-end of my stick. We both lost our balance and landed hard, but he took the worst of it. The ref, sensing a personal issue that would continue, tossed us both out of the game. Through the dual ejection, I had neutralized the best player on the other team, and I was again treated to a hero's welcome as I skated off the rink. After smoking a joint in the nearby woods, I sat down behind my team's bench and watched the rest of the game. We lost 5–2.

AFTER THE game, everyone else drove away. But the Dog and I walked home with our heavy hockey bags. This was because my parents took away my car keys after I was caught smoking a joint with the Dog two nights earlier. Turning the corner onto my street, I saw Hockey Rocky standing in his driveway with a few of his teammates. They stared at us in silence as the Dog and I approached.

Rocky came down his driveway to meet me. He said something stupid like, "Duffy, you started something and I'm going to finish it."

The Dog, a veritable font of *Rocky* movie lines said, "What's shaping up is a classic battle between the Caveman and the Cavalier." Either the Dog didn't understand or didn't care that I was about to get the shit kicked out of me—I assume the latter. Shifting into the voice of *Rocky* villain, Clubber Lang (Mr. T), the Dog announced, "My prediction for the fight—PAIN!" Then the Dog taunted Rocky a little more in his Mr. T voice, "Hey, Italian Scallion. He's gonna hurt you, real bad! Duffy's gonna beat you like a dog."

I dropped my hockey bag behind me. Before I turned to face Rocky, a heavy blow landed on the back of my head that knocked me on all fours. I stood up and charged into Rocky's midsection, catching him with a double-leg takedown. We tumbled to the ground with me on top, but he was too big to hold down. Soon we were both up, breathing heavily and staring at each other.

He faked with his left, and hit me just above the ear with his right. I rocked slightly forward, and was met squarely with a blow on the nose—which started bleeding. I fired back and landed a shot to his chest and a glancing blow to his head. He grinned and said, "Is that all you got?"

He then rocked me again with a hard shot to my jaw. I felt it become unhinged and warm blood flowed into my mouth. I coughed as blood dripped down my throat.

It continued like this for a few more minutes. The blood from my nose was all over both of us, particularly his fists and my shirt. I buried my head into his chest and attempted another takedown, but he leaned forward, putting too much distance between my arms and the back of his knees. He landed a few short, powerful blows to the back of my head until I fell to the ground in front of him.

The Dog, unwilling to let the ass-kicking of his best friend interfere with a good wisecrack, took the opportunity to shout, "He's gonna kick your ass, Hockey Rocky." Everyone laughed, even Rocky and me, at the impossibility of that statement. I stood up again, and he gave me a strong shove with both hands that knocked me back down. He said, "Stay down, Duffy." I did.

———•—•———

THE DOG carried my hockey bag to my house, and I slinked in and showered without letting my folks see me. To my amazement, I came out of the shower looking like nothing ever happened, save a mouse on my jaw that could be plausibly passed off as hockey-related. After my parents went to bed, I washed my bloodstained shirt and it came out okay.

The jaw was another matter. I couldn't close it on one side, and it was terribly sensitive to even the lightest touch. It was a week before I could sleep without waking up in pain a few hours later, and another week before I could truly chew. In those two weeks, I ate a lot of yogurt and lost eight pounds.

In male circles, fights with lopsided outcomes can realign everything. This particular ass-kicking did not. Hockey Rocky was still a slow-witted outsider and a Flyers fan. In some unstated way, we all understood that there was something about Rocky's near-certain use of steroids that tainted his victory. I never antagonized him again, and we gave him more room when we passed each other at the 7-Eleven or Dusal's pizzeria. But Rocco did not press his victory. He continued to exit quickly from chance encounters, particularly when Kevin Kopf, my toughest friend, was around. Mostly, Rocky ceased to exist.

The fight, which the Dog named the "Thrilla on Barzilla"—we lived on Barzilla Road—ended my love of scrapping. As children, most boys fight and no one gets hurt. By the later teen years, only a few boys still fight because getting socked in the mouth can really hurt. The bout with Rocky taught me that I belonged on the bookish side of this divide. I was not going to keep up with the scrappers if it meant eating magic pills and working the heavy bag to *Rocky* music. The path of the wisecracking underachiever was safer and easier.

As for Rocky, he graduated from St. Joe's, which I suspect was no easy task for him, and went on to work in his uncle's landscaping business.

A couple of years after college, I saw Rocky while I was visiting my parents. He was supervising a small crew of Mexicans as they pruned and weeded his parents' yard. From two houses away, I watched Rocky scold a pudgy crew member for dumping a wheelbarrow of mulch in the wrong spot.

Rocky shouted, "Roberto es gordo y feo." He then shoved the man backward on his ass. Seeing that, I felt some vindication for being such a dick to Rocky. I walked toward him, looked at him, and shook my head disapprovingly; he walked away.

Rocco moved out of Morganville many years ago and returned to the Philly suburbs. Two years ago, Kevin Kopf emailed me a local newspaper story about Rocco getting into trouble for tax evasion.

DISCUSSION WITH LISA:

Lisa began the session by asking me a few questions about the writing process. After getting only one word answers, she took a different approach.

"Why are you writing stories about people who were not central to your teen life? You've told me that your best living friends from high school are [she paused to check her notes] Patrick McGowan and Kevin Kopf, and I know nothing about them. And we're really here to discuss the suicide of your best friend from high school, yet you choose to tell me about the peripheral characters in your life."

If I was being honest, I would have said: "Well, Lisa, I think that your profession is quackery. I'm here only because my wife wants me to do this. So you get paid $125 a week to read my stories and tell me I'm not writing about the right people. Screw you." Instead, I offered a more diplomatic and less sincere response, "I don't feel like I'm ready to talk to you about certain people and events. It's easier for me to write about Bobby Flannery and Hockey Rocky."

Lisa leaned forward, "I find it interesting that in this story you wrote about getting your comeuppance. Could you have written this story before our sessions started?"

"Sure."

"Do you think you are learning anything from our sessions?"

I pounced on the question, "I am learning two things. First, I am learning how to write a short story. Second, I am learning the meager buying power of $125 in the psychiatric profession."

Lisa pushed back. "Please shelve the humor. Why do you think I'm asking you about what you might have learned from these sessions?"

I shrugged. She straightened her back—George Washington on his white horse. "Tell me why the story about Rocco is different from the story about Bobby."

I sensed her displeasure, but kept pressing her buttons anyway. I turned on my best Brooklyn-Italian accent, "Because he's a *paisan* of yours, Dr. Melfi, and you don't like me taking shots at the fine Italian people."

"Maybe I am *your* Jennifer Melfi, but you are not *my* Tony Soprano. I asked . . ."

But I spoke over her in my Brooklyn-Italian accent, "Ya know, Dr. Melfi, I don't look much like Tony S. from Jersey, but I do resemble my goombah friend Rocco D'Alessio from Philly. You can call me 'Mussels Marinara,' the Italian strongman."

"Cute. But not exactly correct. Remember that my name is Moscovitz. I am nobody's paisan. Let's try again. How is this story different than the first?"

I knew what she wanted to hear, and having extracted my pound of flesh, I was ready to give her what she wanted. "Okay, this story's different because I get my ass-kicked. I am a bully, *and* a victim."

Lisa put down her notepad, "I'm glad you said that."

"Why do you think it's such a big deal?"

"Because your story with Rocky reflects a complicated human relationship—not just a bully picking on an unfortunate victim. If you wrote these two stories to prove to me that you were a very *bad* boy in high school, you can check that off your list now. I believe you were a *bad* boy. Why is it so important for you to demonstrate this to me?"

I thought for a minute, "Well, I thought the purpose of these stories was to help us figure out if I was mean enough to move my best friend toward suicide. The bullying of Bobby and Rocco shows you that."

"Okay. You've shown me two victims of your bullying. Do you want to explore something else in your next story?"

"Like what?" I asked.

"What about girls? Did you attend high school with any girls?"

"Yes, but I bullied boys." I rocked in the rocking chair a couple of times, thinking about her question and what I might write about. Then I understood her suggestion.

5

Fran from Brooklyn

I was always bored in high school. I don't think I could name a single high school course where I didn't daydream through class, with the exception of sophomore Biology, taught by the sexy Ms. Hill. I passed the time rubbing myself with a hand inside my jeans pocket and wishing I was anywhere else. I also doodled, sometimes on paper, and sometimes on the desk. One day shortly after the Dog started me listening to Joe Jackson, I scribbled a song lyric—"Everything gives you cancer"—on a desk in room A-117, for no particular reason.

The next day, my jaw dropped when I saw that someone had written, "There's no cure, there's no answer." This was the next line of the Joe Jackson song. In this pre-Internet era, there was no way that the writer of this line could have researched my quote and responded so quickly. This writer knew "Cancer," a Latin-influenced piano song from side two of a poor-selling Joe Jackson album. In culturally stagnant Morganville High School, the only person who knew about Joe Jackson was the Dog, but the Dog confirmed that he did not have class in A-117. We were intrigued.

The next day, I tried something else. I scribbled on that same desk in A-117, "Well, the toilet went crazy yesterday afternoon, the plumber he says never flush a tampoon!" The mystery respondent knew Joe Jackson, but there was no chance he'd know Frank

Zappa's "Flakes" (a nutty song cycle about incompetent trades-people taking Zappa's money). But the next day, there was the response, "This great information cost me half a week's pay, and the toilet blew up later on the next day."

Next to the response was a personal note, "Zappa is excellent, and so is this game." There was also a challenge back to me, "And if California slides into the ocean, like those mystics and statistics say it will."

I was stumped, and so was the Dog. The annoyed Dog suggested, "Our mystery writer is nothing but a poet-wannabe quoting himself." I scribbled four question marks next to the confounding lyric and waited for an answer.

The reply was there the next day, "And if California slides into the ocean, like those mystics and statistics say it will . . . I predict this motel will be standing, until I've paid my bill." There was some additional information and a question, "'Desperadoes Under the Eaves,' Warren Zevon. What's your name?"

I replied, "Matt McDuff Duffy, Junior. Who are you?"

I received only a cryptic reply, "Fran from Brooklyn."

"We don't know any guy named Fran. And Fran is a pretty panty-waist name for any guy who listens to Zappa." The Dog frowned.

"Fran could be a girl."

"Don't be such a douche, McDuff. Do you really think Francine Niños is capable of winning an obscure lyrics contest? Do you think *any* girl in Morganville High School listens to Joe Jackson or Frank Zappa?"

The Dog was not sexist in the classic sense, but he observed, "Morganville girls are deliberately raised by their parents to be empty-headed—consequently, they are." (If Jane Goodall studied the chimps of Morganville High School, she would have concluded the same thing.) At the Dog's suggestion, I checked the high school yearbook for clues on "Fran from Brooklyn." No help.

AND SO began our mini-quest to find out about "Fran from Brooklyn." We sent out pleas for information to everyone. The initial intelligence was bad and we were directed down various dead-end paths, including a depressing conversation with a sophomore doofus named Frank who believed that Sammy Hagar yelling "I can't drive 55" was a great lyric.

Then, just as interest was waning, we received a promising lead through Kevin Kopf. "The mysterious Fran from Brooklyn is probably Francine Miglino, a girl whose family relocated from Brooklyn last summer." Kevin's description of her was tantalizing, "I don't know her. But Carrie Wilner tells me that your Fran-from-Brooklyn dresses like a punk-rocker, and puts down 'popular' girls. She tells everyone how much she *hates* Morganville High School."

My heart skipped while listening to Kevin's report. The Dog was instantly jealous. He grunted, "I cannot name a single good thing that ever came out of Brooklyn."

I learned that Fran was in A-117 during last period. I cut my final class and conducted a surveillance of the class as it exited. Finding a person dressed like a punk in Morganville High School was pretty easy, and easier still because she was the first person to jet out of class when the bell rang. I watched her walk away: she wore tight vinyl pants wrapped around a perfect ass and a T-shirt with crazy shit pinned to it. She had long black hair with shaved sides like Annabella Lwin, the super-hot singer from Bow Wow Wow.[1]

I needed to meet her.

STARTING JUNIOR year, standard practice in Morganville High School was to deliver detention reminder notices to the lucky individuals during the last period of the school day. Upon receipt, those students headed directly to detention in the cafeteria. Though hated by all teachers with last period classes, this practice curbed the once rampant problem of kids skipping detention.

---

1. Bow Wow Wow recorded a few moderately popular albums in the early '80s that combined Punk Rock with eye candy for teen boys.

A year earlier, I had stolen a small pile of blank detention notices from the office (stolen for spite—I never expected that they'd be useful for anything). But now I had the chance to fill out a detention notice and pull Fran from Brooklyn out of class in a bad-ass way. I imagined Fran from Brooklyn appreciating my daring and originality. She would confess to love at first sight, and then we'd make out in the high school hallway. What could go wrong?

The next day, a few minutes into last period, I knocked on the door of A-117. This was twenty minutes before the notices were usually distributed, but I was too anxious to wait. I entered the room and waved the notice. I called, "Francine," and leaned against the doorway, trying to look cool.

The always gruff Mrs. Bean glared at me, "Why are you so early?" I shrugged.

Mrs. Bean motioned for Fran to leave with me. Fran started to protest by saying, "This is bullsh—," but caught herself before completing the taboo word. She then matter-of-factly stated, "I do not have detention, this is a mistake." Mrs. Bean rolled her eyes. Fran mumbled, "Great. I'm getting screwed again." She gathered up her books, and came toward me in a huff.

Once in the hallway together, we started walking towards the cafeteria. Fran started in on me, "I have done nothing to earn a detention in two months—at least nothing anyone knows about, and I'm really pissed off about this screw-up." I could feel the heat in her voice; then she went quiet. My plan was unraveling.

Only twenty feet from the cafeteria entrance, I dialed up some courage and confessed, "Um . . . uh . . . Francine, I am the guy you have been exchanging lyrics with at my, uh your, um, my desk. I, um . . . thought you might want to . . . um, um . . . meet me."

She looked me up and down, "I imagined you'd look *very* different." The disappointment on my face must have shown. After a few seconds, she offered up a consolation line, "But I really like the lyric game. Let's keep doing that."

FRAN'S PUNK-ROCK attire sold her short. She played violin, figure-skated, and read novels not assigned in school. The first time she told me she was reading a novel for kicks—I think it was Tom Robbins' *Even Cowgirls Get the Blues*—I thought she was bull-shitting me. She had a diverse collection of records and cassettes, including Punk, but ranging into the intelligent, lyric-driven rock of Ray Davies, Warren Zevon, and Leonard Cohen. She also listened to folk music from the Inca Mountains and Eastern Europe, and was listening to South African "township music" long before Paul Simon's *Graceland* album.

Over the next few months, Fran from Brooklyn and I became friends. We continued writing notes back and forth to each other and exchanging lyrics. I invited her out several times, but she always said no. After a few gentle brush-offs she told me, "I have a boyfriend in Brooklyn. He's a starving actor by day and a night club bouncer at night. I spend every weekend with him." She showed me a little picture of a husky guy with slicked-back hair and tattoos, and ended the conversation by saying, "I'm going to move in with Billy the day after I leave prison in Morganville." As a senior, her sentence would be a short one.

In school, however, Fran happily started hanging out with my friends and me. Fran told great stories about getting into trouble for being smarter than her teachers. One example was the shouting match with her Biology teacher over the "greatest leap in evolution." Here's how she narrated the incident: "The stupid Ms. Oberweiss stated that 'the greatest evolutionary leap was from rodents to primates and humans because of the advance in brain power.' I stood up and told her, 'That's a very anthropocentric position.' She then challenged me to offer my thoughts on the greatest evolutionary leap. So I did. I told the class: 'The greatest evolutionary leap was from squid-like sea creatures to fish because of the development of the backbone. And, more importantly, animals finally stopped eating and shitting out of the same hole.' I earned two days detention for the subversion."

Like me, the womanizing Kevin Kopf loved Fran. He called her "forbidden fruit" and showed her a level of respect not given to any other girl. Even twenty years later, when we drink together, we talk about her. More than once, Kevin's said, "Francine was the only girl in Morganville who was out of my league."

The Dog was another matter. He'd speak to Fran in an over-the-top Brooklyn accent and ask, "Is it true that Brooklyn is really Islanders' country?" (Only Flyers' fans are lower than New York Islanders' fans, assuming there are any Islanders fans at all.) When the Dog and Fran met in school, the Dog would say in a cranky AM talk-radio voice, "And now on the line, we have a first-time caller, Fran from Brooklyn." He'd taunt Fran sexually, asking her, "Do you like to do it Doggy style?" and then bark at her.

Fran always had an appropriate retort about the Dog's "pre-pubescent penis" or his "persistent-to-chronic virginity." One time the Dog taunted Fran, "When you kiss your boyfriend, do you think about me?" Fran responded, "Ya, that happened once—and my vag went dry for a week." Once, when speaking privately to me, Fran called the Dog "that sad, little puppy." At the time, I had no idea why.

Fran called our love of hockey "quaint" and concluded, "I like you boys, but you suffer from amniopia." As if to confirm the accuracy of her judgment, no one ever bothered to look up the word.[2]

———•———

TRUE TO her word, Fran moved to New York City the weekend following graduation. I never had a chance to say goodbye to her properly. The last time I saw her I was raging at the Dog; Fran intervened to defuse the violent situation. The last thing I ever heard her say was in the form of a directive to Kevin Kopf about me: "McDuff's out of control, get him out of here."

The day after that incident, Fran gave Kevin a small package with my name on it. There was no note. Inside the package was a baseball cap that read, "I snatch kisses, and vice versa," and a

---

2. Commonly referred to as lazy eye, amniopia is the medical term for the inability to see three-dimensionally.

T-shirt with a creepy picture of Patti Smith that read, "I don't fuck much with the past, but I fuck plenty with the future." There was also a cassette tape. That tape remade my musical tastes. Side one contained songs from a few '70s not-quite-Punk bands (Television, Jonathan Richman and the Modern Lovers, Talking Heads). Side two was also filled with songs from the '70s, but folksy, Celtic bands (Steeleye Span, Pentangle, Fairport Convention). Today, I consider myself the lone member of the New Jersey chapter of the Steeleye Span fan club.

I made a couple of lame attempts after graduation to find Fran. I received an address from a supposed friend of hers and mailed a letter. I did not get a reply. A few years later I tried to find her via directory assistance with no luck. While writing this book, I Googled her name, and then checked Facebook and various directory assistance websites. Acknowledging my Internet limitations, I had my son Jack dork around the Internet to see if he could find any information on her. We found nothing.

Fran's current whereabouts and circumstances are unknown to me.

DISCUSSION WITH LISA:

I headed into Lisa's office to discuss "Fran from Brooklyn" with nervous excitement, like a young artist before his first showing.

As I entered, Lisa asked, "Did it feel good writing about that perfect girl from high school?"

I nodded yes.

"You really had a crush on her, didn't you?"

"I wasn't the only one, but yes. It was impossible not to be a big fan of Francine."

"Your friend, the Dog, was not a fan of hers, was he?"

I was surprised that Lisa could be so wrong, "Sure he was. He was just too much of a dick to show it. She even saved his ass after he treated her horribly for months on end, though I didn't discuss that in this story. Even today, that's a very raw memory."

I paused to see if Lisa would let me skate by without discussing that incident. Lisa looked at me as if to say, "Fine, take a pass on this *for now*."

I thought some more about the Dog and his relationship with Francine. Then the words to describe the Dog just tumbled out. "The Dog treated people well inversely to how much he respected them. He probably had a bigger crush on Francine than I did. That's why he treated her so badly."

"What does that say about you being the Dog's best friend?" Lisa asked.

It was as if a giant neon sign started flashing over her head: BREAKTHROUGH MOMENT AHEAD! I knew what I was supposed to say, and I was ready to say it. "It means that the Dog thought I was a piece of shit. He thought I was his easily manipulated second-fiddle. I was more of a plaything to him than a friend."

I felt a chill go up my neck. On some level, I always knew this was true of my relationship with the Dog, but had never dared to state it, even to myself. "I get why I wasn't torn up when the Dog died."

I looked into the faux-fire a few feet away and asked, "Do you want to read about how I lost my virginity?"

6

The Aptly Named Jeannie Small

The summer before junior year, on whatever Friday and Saturday nights there were no parties, the default activity was meeting at Dukakis's Eyebrows, a small clearing of land with a concrete slab a quarter mile into the woods behind Freedom Tree Park. At the entrance to the clearing were two overgrown hedges that vaguely resembled the bushy eyebrows of our first Mediterranean-American presidential candidate, Mike Dukakis— hence the name. No one ever figured out what the county parks people were thinking a few years earlier when they poured a slab of cement and planted hedges in the middle of the woods. But the taxpayers of Monmouth County could take solace in knowing that at least my friends and I made great use of it, complementing the slab with a fire-pit and a lean-to we made with a tarp stolen from the park. It was further augmented with a hodge-podge of lawn furniture lifted from the backyards of our least favorite people in Battleview Acres. In time, we decorated the site with dozens of beer and liquor bottles, crushed Styrofoam fast-food sandwich boxes, and Pringle's canisters.

Inevitably, word of Dukakis's Eyebrows spread outside my circle of friends. Kevin and I suspected the Dog of leaking the location, but he emphatically denied it, calling us "a couple of dickheads" for even suggesting it.

That fall, a large clique of seniors, more or less led by Andy van Mater, discovered Dukakis's Eyebrows and started hanging out with us there. Andy—nicknamed AVM—was descended from one of the Dutch families that first settled Monmouth County in the late 1600s. He and his friends lived in the village of Wickatunk, which predated the migration of thousands of New Yorkers and the subsequent suburbanization of greater Morganville. The Wick-atunk kids were authentic Jersey rednecks, and because of that, would not smoke pot. But they drank huge amounts of cheap beer and carried firearms. After drinking heavily, they loved to blow away beer bottles, squirrels, and NO-HUNTING signs. Their brand of bad-ass had real authenticity.

Despite differences in age and culture, AVM and his associated seniors respectfully shared Dukakis's Eyebrows with us. We gained patron relationships with a group of shit-kicking seniors, which was kind of cool. Each week, AVM requested, "Hey, New York boys, do something funny." We would.

Andy took a particular liking to me. He'd call out, "McDuff, tell me your latest about hooky or hockey." The Dog noted Andy's fondness for me, with comments along the lines of "pull your nose out of AVM's ass" and "you've got corn in your teeth from kissing his ass." This was probably a little bit true. The Dog once said to Andy, "You know McDuff's mom is Puerto Rican. Better watch your hubcaps." The Dog passed this off as a joke, but I really think he was banking on AVM's bigotry (we assumed all rednecks were bigots) to drive a wedge between us.

AVM's clique of seniors included four girls, all with conveniently descriptive names or nicknames. There was the butch and vulgar Melissa Offerman (pronounced "off her man"); the nearly as butch and even more vulgar Deirdre "The Bull" Dozier; Robin "Red Breasts" Carney (well known for sunbathing topless); and the tiny and smart-mouthed, Jeannie Small. They were not girls suburban parents characterized as "nice." Def Leopard and AC/DC concert shirts dominated their wardrobes, they cursed constantly, and they chain-smoked cigarettes.

One night as they were swearing up a storm, I appointed myself the "potty-mouth cop" and started spinning my hands atop my head while imitating a police siren after each swear word. AVM loved it. Soon, all the guys were doing it.

Of the four, Jeannie Small was the best of the bunch. Urged by AVM, I was paired up with her on weekly booze runs. She had a car and I was five-eleven with a mustache. Despite being only sixteen, I passed tolerably well for twenty-one in dimly lit redneck bars where no one cared much about age anyway.

Jeannie drove like a maniac in her father's old Lincoln—a giant car with a permanent muffler problem. She swerved in and out of traffic, gunned it at red lights, and yipped like the lovable redneck, Bo Duke, every time she passed a truck by flooring it up the highway shoulder. From the outside, it appeared like no one was driving the car, and the cigarette smoke wisping from the driver's window was more easily detected than her tiny body inside the massive cockpit. Jeannie scared the shit out of me, but I respected the fact that in a world of posers, she was genuinely dangerous.

Jeannie knew that a nice suburban boy must do anything, no matter how dumb, just because she requested it. On her dares and demands, I started stealing various signs she identified as cool or funny. Our heists included: a purple triangle that read TEMPORARY SIGN from a new subdivision site, the NO HUNTING—CHILDREN MAY BE PRESENT sign from Thompson Park, and my favorite, PLANNED PARENTHOOD—USE REAR ENTRANCE. Once we drove into Rahway, a rough town a half-hour north of Morganville, just to steal the amusingly handwritten MUST PAY IN VANCE sign from a gas station. The Pakistani owner chased us briefly with a tire iron as we sped away. With McGowan's dad's bolt-cutters, a joint from the Dog, and a crazy little girl in a giant Lincoln, no interesting sign in central New Jersey was safe.

A strange friendship grew between Jeannie and me. We never said anything nice to each other, and often put each other down in front of others. She made fun of my slight lisp, and endlessly repeated the qualifying phrase, "to a certain extent," after she heard me use it to answer the question, "Are you drunk?" She set up people to ask me embarrassing questions and then responded for me—"Q: Hey McDuff, does your asshole hurt from taking it up the butt?" A: "To a certain extent." As for me, I never let up on her four-eleven, eighty-five-pound body—calling her "the Aptly Named Jeannie Small." The name stuck. Everyone started calling her the Aptly Named Jeannie Small—eventually shortened to "Aptly Named" and then just "Aptly." Despite this, neither of us felt put off; the barbs were always blunted by eye contact and a smile or giggle.

We returned from liquor runs with me carrying two cases of beer and a sign balanced on top, Jeannie carrying two fifths of Jack Daniels. We poured shots of Jack into our beers after the first sip to spike the alcohol content. Andy always praised us and declared Jeannie and me "a great team." The stories of our sign thefts were retold again and again at Dukakis's Eyebrows, each time with more fantastic details. Jeannie freely embellished the facts, particularly with regard to my supposed narrow escapes from rabid dogs, shotgun-firing rednecks from the rival town of Howell, and "the Uzi-toting Pakistani gas station owner" in Rahway. I played along.

By November, Dukakis's Eyebrows was spinning out of control. More and more seniors started showing up, including a group of boisterous jocks who were not subject to AVM's mellowing influence. For a while, the originals continued coming, but we left by ten PM after too many jocks showed up, depleted the liquor supply, and proclaimed themselves "blasted" after their second beer.

One November evening, we left Dukakis's Eyebrows early after half the varsity football team showed up. After AVM and his boys drove off, the four girls, the Dog, and I drifted over to the park swings. The Dog passed around two joints and the girls passed around a bottle of Jack.

I put myself on one of the swings, and started swinging gently. Jeannie stood at the end of my arc putting a joint in my mouth on top of one arc, and then withdrawing it on my next swing. We did this for a while; it was pretty funny. After the joint was done, Jeannie started poking at me on each swing, asking if I "liked going up down." The pokes moved south; she started grabbing at my crotch. The Dog called Jeannie a "skank" and walked off. So there I was, alone and hammered with three girls I disliked, and Jeannie, who was grossing me out.

I decided to exit the situation with some panache. I swung higher and harder making it impossible for Jeannie to grab at me. Near the top of a particularly high swing I launched myself into the air. I landed heavily on one leg and tumbled ass-over-head before settling on my back. Three of the girls came over to see if I was okay, Jeannie did not.

Fortunately, besides a sore ankle, I was fine. I straightened up, and dusted myself off. I said, "It's past my bedtime" and started for home.

Turning the corner onto Barzilla Road, I noticed Jeannie following me. As I reached the back door of my house, she came up behind me. We didn't say a word to each other as she entered the house with me.

My house had a small semi-finished basement which was mostly for the washer and dryer, but included a little den area. It wasn't much: an old couch, an older easy chair, and a television set with a horizontal-hold problem. It was impossible to watch the TV for more than ten minutes without the people on the screen careening upward into oblivion and then reappearing at the bottom. The basement was always a little damp and the easy chair always piled with laundry. I slept off my rough nights here.

We sat next to each other on the couch. Jeannie told me about a horse her parents had bought for her when she was fourteen, and then took away as punishment when she refused to stop seeing an older boyfriend. "Then that dick, Derrick, dumped me hard. He told me he was not attracted to me. He said I have the body of a little girl. My asshole parents were happy about it."

She started to sob, "I am stuck with the boobs of a twelve-year-old." As her sobs turned into crying I put my arm around her and her head slid onto my chest. I felt saltwater and mucus seep through my shirt onto my chest. I tried to joke, telling her, "Jeannie, you are saddened equally by two unloving parents and two little boobies. There's a karmic duality to your problems."

The joke bombed. Jeannie gave me a puzzled look, then said, "McDuff, you are the weirdest guy I know. Why do I like you?"

I swallowed hard and didn't say anything else, but I gave her a box of tissues and patted her head. Slouching into the couch pillows, I nodded off as she continued talking about her miserable life.

I woke up to Jeannie laying on top of me. We kissed several times; she tasted like old beer sucked off a furnace floor. She unbuttoned my pants, joked, "Now who's the aptly named small," and rubbed me. Fortunately, I was in the hands of a very competent individual, and my shortcoming was rectified. She pulled down her pants and climbed over me. In a few minutes it was over for both of us. We lay alongside each other without saying anything.

Finally, I whispered, "You can't stay."

Jeannie looked away. "I know." She pulled on her panties and pants, and went to the bathroom. I was asleep before she left the house.

———

With the demise of Dukakis's Eyebrows, Jeannie and I rarely saw each other. When we did, I remember feeling a little bit sick and trying to avoid her, but without giving her an obvious brush-off. Once at a party during my senior year, Jeannie sent Deirdre Dozier over. "The Bull" asked me to come outside and smoke a joint with them. I declined saying, "As a recent convert to

Mormonism, I am now living clean. Just ask either of my eleven-year-old wives."

That was the one and only time Jeannie tried to re-engage me. She moved out of New Jersey a few years later with a much older guy (a cop, I am told) and I lost track of her. I once heard from Kevin that Jeannie was in Florida. She had two babies from two dads, never married, and never had a real job. But she was doing just fine financially due to a big insurance settlement from a car accident. The other driver was judged at fault after he blew a higher score than Jeannie on the Breathalyzer.

While conducting research for this book, I corroborated Kevin's information. I found a short article about Jeannie's car accident, excerpted from the Jacksonville *Sentinel,* on a drunk-driving prevention website. The article noted that the accident occurred at one forty-five AM on a Saturday in 1998. Jeannie's six- and three-year-old children were in the car at the time. The younger child was in a car seat that was not properly secured, and was badly injured when Jeannie's car was sideswiped by the drunk driver. At the time of the article, the child was in intensive care. Neither driver was seriously hurt.

I still find myself wondering why Jeannie was driving around with her small children at one forty-five on a Saturday night.

DISCUSSION WITH LISA:

Lisa started by asking, "You seem to have made a point of ending your story by noting that Jeannie Small is in Florida and probably not doing all that well. Why?"

"Oh, I don't know. Mostly I was just making the point that she's white trash."

Lisa frowned, "Do you think this is an appropriate figure of speech?"

Seeing that the term white trash got under Lisa's skin, I decided to press her political correctness buttons. "Don't worry, Lisa. Poor whites are the last group of Americans we can pre-judge and diss without catching any heat. It is perfectly acceptable to call a group of rural white people rednecks or hicks or crackers. Say Negro or Kike and look out. Comedy careers like that of Larry the Cable Guy are built on making fun of white trash, and it's pretty damn funny. So, I think I can say white trash. If James Carville—top advisor to a president—can joke about waving a twenty-dollar bill in a trailer park to get people to lie about sleeping with the president, certainly I can have some fun in the same space."

We argued for the next twenty minutes about the PC double standard that exists for poor, rural whites. Finally, Lisa called off the discussion, "Fine, let's agree to disagree. It's time to discuss this week's story. Why did you choose Jeannie Small and this particular story?"

I spoke too glibly, "After 'Fran from Brooklyn,' I didn't want you thinking I was a fag."

Lisa remained expressionless, but I heard annoyance in her voice, "Archie Bunker has not been funny since the '70s. You need to update your comic persona." She asked again, "What brought this person and this story into your head now?"

I knew the answer to Lisa's question, but didn't want to say it. Lisa waited. I waited too. I thought, "This chick's pretty smart. She knows I am hiding something."

After about a minute of this test of wills, I caved, "I picked this story because I went all the way with this girl, albeit clumsily, and then walked away from her. I needed *you* to see this. I wanted you to see that I walked away from her. I was not always the loser."

"Do you consider Francine and Jeannie the most important women from your high school years?"

"No, Francine was my greatest crush, but she was transient. Jeannie Small was just a dismal girl who happened to be the first notch on the bedpost. I need to, no I want to, tell you about the girl from high school who became an important friend."

7

'L'

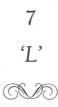

In addition to McGowan, Kevin, and the Dog, I had two other good friends in high school—the arch-slacker Dan Mueller, my lab partner, and his best friend, Bob Strimple. We loved Mueller and Strimple, but they were denied "inner circle" status because they didn't play hockey and they lived on the other side of the park, in the fancy subdivision of Excelsior Oaks.

Mueller was a big guy with huge hands. He had a gift for misbehaving in class and teachers thinking it cute. For example, he once started clapping fifteen minutes into Chemistry class and then said loudly, "Wow! What a great class today, that's a wrap." Then he started putting away his books noisily. I would have been nailed with detention for the same stunt. Strimple was voted the senior class clown, proving that he was both funny and afforded popular crowd status, despite not behaving like a member of the popular crowd.

Mueller and Strimple thought I was some combination of funny, interesting, and pitiful, particularly after I told them the way I lost my virginity to Jeannie Small. Walking out of Chemistry class one day, Mueller declared, "Dr. Robert Strimple and I will take on the most daring scientific experiment ever—getting McDuff properly laid."

I didn't like being the subject of their "scientific experiment," but liked them enough to play along. Every few days, I received updates on the women they were lining up to meet me at a small party that Strimple would host. I thought they were bullshitting me. Then, on a freezing cold Saturday in February, Strimple invited me to a small party at his house for the sole purpose of getting me "properly laid."

THAT SATURDAY night, I went to Strimple's without telling anyone. This earned me a Charlie Horse and Wet-Willy from Kevin at the Sunday hockey game. It was a small party—Mueller, Strimple, and me with seven or eight girls, including their current girlfriends. The party lacked beer, but there were lots of wine coolers—which I took as proof that I was out of my element. Clearly, the girls knew that the purpose of the evening was to determine if I was worthy of dating. I felt their eyes on me the moment I came into the house. I brought a small bottle of Yukon Jack hidden in my jacket pocket; because I was nervous, I took two big swigs in the bathroom a few minutes after arriving. I then drank three or four wine coolers in a half-hour to impress the girls. By ten, I was stupid drunk and forgot all of their names.

I remember only some of what happened next. Here's what I know, with parts of the narrative filled in by Mueller's post-event retelling of my exploits.

I pawed at all five of the available girls. Four of them wanted nothing to do with me. But the fifth gave me the benefit of the doubt. I remember sitting in an easy chair, grabbing her by the back belt-loop, and pulling her toward me several times. On one of these pulls she turned, fell on top of me, and we kissed. Then we paired up alone on an old couch in Strimple's basement and fooled around. This went well enough, I suppose, because our tops came off.

At some point, I started feeling sick and ran off to vomit. I didn't know my way around Strimple's house and did not find a bathroom. But I did find the back door and ran outside. I stretched across the air conditioner and vomited into a frozen flower bed.

Before I was done, everyone at the party was watching me through the bay window in the living room.

I was told that by the time I came back in, my chest and back were bright red from cold exposure, and I was shivering. The girl from the couch in the basement dressed herself and came upstairs. I remember her taking me to a bathroom and handing me a washcloth with warm water so I could clean my face. She then brought me into the kitchen, and un-playfully slapped Strimple in the head when he started imitating my heaves. She fed me teaspoons of hot chocolate. After a few teaspoons, she gave me the mug and I took a large sip. This prompted an eruption of new vomiting, and puke went all over the kitchen floor. It splashed up on the girl's shoes and pants legs.

I went back downstairs and slept off the rest of the night on Strimple's basement couch.

———

THE NEXT Monday morning in school I told what I could remember of this story to Kevin as we exited homeroom. The gaps in my memory awaited Mueller's debriefing, which I hoped would happen during Chemistry class that afternoon. Walking down the hall I passed Mueller's girlfriend, Dana, and another girl. The other girl looked at me intently, and whispered something to Dana.

They giggled. The second girl looked familiar and I deduced she was the girl from Strimple's couch. I looked back at her and nodded. She nodded back and smiled.

Kevin asked, "What's her name?"

I told him, "I have no f-ing idea." We both laughed and watched her turn left at the end of the hallway.

Kevin concluded, "Her ass is too big, but she has nice tits and you don't need to put a bag over that face. She's not bad." I remember disliking Kevin's cold analysis, even if he was about right.

Mueller's girlfriend found me in the cafeteria that day. She was a "popular girl" and thus took a risk by associating with me in such a public setting. Without saying anything other than a curt

"Hi," she delivered a note from the girl at the party as I stood on the lunch line. It read:

Hi,

Hope you're feeling better. My pants washed clean, so no harm. I will stop by your locker at the end of the day.

L

Mueller missed Chemistry class that day. This induced a wave of panic in me because now I had no way of finding out the mysterious L's name before meeting her. I was not ready to face her.

———————

I SCOOTED out of my last period Algebra II class when the bell rang, and made a beeline for Kevin's car. I shivered for twenty minutes in the cold waiting for Kevin and the Dog to show up. When they did, the Dog said, "Hey ass, we stood by your locker waiting for you for *hours*. Way to go on the communications."

Kevin nodded in agreement, then offered, "Hey, big tits hovered around your locker for ten minutes; she looked pissed-off when she left. I thought about introducing myself, and telling her that you were in the parking lot barfing, but I feel merciful today."

I was stung by the abuse, but laughed it off. "I just came out early to claim 'shotgun.' You're sitting in back today, Dog."

On the ride home, Kevin and I discussed the L-situation in the front seat. We concluded that I liked her enough to do something to get myself back in her good graces. Kevin agreed to take me to the mall to get L a gift. The Dog, following only half the conversation from the backseat, was displeased. He said, "McDuff, you're behaving like a big pussy. Why are you fussing over a fatass sophomore?"

Kevin stuck up for me—sort of. "A trip to the mall is a small sacrifice for a dive in the snatch-patch." The Dog relented; from the backseat he had no choice.

Kevin and the Dog dropped me off at the mall entrance, and drove off toward the back of the nearly empty parking lot. As they rolled away, I saw the Dog pull out a mega-joint that would make Cheech & Chong blush.

I entered the mall. The fake strawberry-perfumed air made me regret it. To this day, I hate the smell of mall air. I had no idea what I was supposed to buy for L, and wandered the near-empty mall before entering a store called something lame like Sweet Reminders. There, I found myself ten feet away from L, who was looking at something that was pink, fluffy, and unrecognizable. We looked at each other. I muttered, "Hi, uhhh . . . L."

She mumbled "Hi," looked away, and walked out into the mall. I weakly called, "Hey." She didn't turn around.

—◆—

I saw L a few more times during my junior year, mostly sightings in the hallway. I tried to strike up a conversation twice, but received only cool one-word responses.

She warmed up to me over the summer. She called me to "express support" after she heard about the Dog, and gave me a hug on the first day of school of my senior year.

We were in the same Psychology elective that fall. The teacher spent most of the first month of school discussing topics like "the grieving process" and "depression in teenagers." I was selected to answer questions too frequently for it to be a coincidence. I made L laugh each time with silly, sympathy-baiting responses like: "I feel a lot of resentment today. Like I want to break the points off 1,000 pencils." Or "Today my head is just so heavy—it will never lift up to see a sunny day again." One day, L sat down next to me, and we passed notes back and forth about what I would say if called upon. When I put my arm around her leaving class, she didn't remove it.

Throughout senior year, L gently rebuffed my many attempts to date her. But she agreed to attend my senior prom with me "as friends." She laughed the whole night, and allowed me to get her high for the first time. L and I did the nasty that night. It wasn't nasty at all. We saw each other nearly every day that summer— and our spontaneous weekend trip to Niagara Falls remains one of my fondest memories. We broke up at the end of the summer because I was going to college three hours away, and we both agreed it was the right thing to do. For the next six years until I married, we flirted with each other, but one of us always had a steady, so we never again rekindled that summer's fling.

—⊷—

LYNETTE HAKE (now Robson) graduated from Morganville High with honors, went to Swarthmore College, and received her Master of Social Work degree from Rutgers. She was a social worker in Newark for several years, then a court-appointed child advocate in Bergen County. In this role she met a young attorney with a big chest and bigger chin, Lawson Robson. She married the guy. With assistance from his old-money WASP relatives and some cosmetic surgery, he became a telegenic victims' rights attorney who now advertises during daytime TV judge shows. His commercials include various poor people repeating the awful catchphrase, "Lawson put the law on my side." Lynette and their three adorable children are important props in the ads. The Robsons now live in Saddle River—a swanky mailing address—in a huge house with a guest cottage. Their guest cottage is the size of my house.

Lynette and I remain friends. She's the only close female friend I've ever had. She re-ignited my love of fiction ten years ago when she gave me a copy of William Golding's *The Inheritors*, and we continue to exchange novels. A few times a year, we see each other for tapas and sangria. Sometimes I bring McGowan along, and the three of us giggle like twelve-year-olds at a sleepover.

Kevin shows no interest in seeing her. He has taunted me, "The 'L' isn't for Lynette, it's for 'Lorena,' as in Lorena Bobbitt— the psycho who cut off her husband's wanger just because he tuned her up once or twice. McDuff, she's done the same to you; she's turned you into a eunuch." The last time I invited Kevin to join us, he responded, "Keep her away from me. I like my balls where they are. I saw yours rolling down the street yesterday afternoon."

Lynette and I have met for dinner with our spouses a few times. When we did, everyone was on his or her best behavior, so none of these meetings are noteworthy. Because both spouses are uncomfortable about our twenty-year friendship, the conversation was stiff and the laughter fake. It's now an unwritten rule that spouses are not invited when we meet.

For the record, I think Lynette's husband is a dickhead. I have every reason to believe that the love has drained away between them. She doesn't complain too much to me about him, but has joked with me about "suffering from chronic affluenza," and once mockingly referred to him as "my husband, the celebrity attorney." I poke fun at his Mayflower lineage and pudgy TV image, calling him "the bloated attorney, Upton Pumpaloaf IV," and she laughs. I think she stays with him out of a sense of obligation to the children—her youngest is only nine. He stays with her because a messy divorce from his sinless wife might smudge his carefully cultivated public image—to say nothing of losing fifty percent of his assets.

A few years ago, Lynette won some kind of award for her volunteerism on behalf of an affordable housing coalition. The honor generated an article about her in the Bergen Record, her county newspaper, with a picture of her posing with the award. The gravity of the award is proven by Lynette's picture beating out the installation of speed bumps at the local skate rink for above-the-fold coverage on page one.

When I emailed the article to Kevin, he replied, "She used to be L, now she's XL." This was a reference to Lynette's significant weight gain since high school. Kevin's a dear old friend, but sometimes he's a dick.

DISCUSSION WITH LISA:

Mt. Rushmore looked just a little bit warmer as I entered the office. Settling into the rocking chair, I said, "I knew you'd like this one. With this story, you finally have a chance to see me as something other than a monster."

"I never saw you as a monster." Lisa looked down and shifted in her seat, then added, "But talk to me about Lynette and your continued friendship with her. Has it impacted your relationship with your family?"

I sucked in some air and then spoke bluntly, "I never even mention Lynette's name in front of Diane. It eats away at Diane to know Lynette and I are still close. And it irritates me that I have to tell Diane that I'm going out with McGowan or staying late at the office on the nights when I see Lynette. Diane's just not rational about this, and it limits how I think about my wife." I paused, surprised at what I just said.

Then I pushed forward. "Lynette is the *only* woman with whom I have a mature friendship. I love Diane; she's a devoted mother and a partner in my life. But I don't think Diane and I really are *friends*."

"Would you ever share this story with Lynette or Diane?"

I responded with a resounding, "Hell no—not either of them."

There was a pause. "Do you *love* Lynette?"

I gasped, "Married men don't talk about loving any fat chicks other than their wives. I don't care if you're my shrink or not. I am not going to answer that question." I stated this with as much gravity as I could muster in hopes of pushing Lisa to a new topic.

Lisa paused. "Fine. If you were not married, would there be some likelihood that you'd have feelings toward Lynette?"

I exhaled, "Yes."

We digressed briefly into a discussion of "thought crimes"— those little sins we commit every day, but only in our heads. We discussed whether or not they are inevitable and even healthy. Finally, Lisa pushed back in her chair. "Any other girls you want to write about?"

"No, after Lynette there's not much more for me to say about my teen misadventures with the ladies. Instead, I think I'm going to tell you about a boy I befriended, and how he was worse off for it."

8

Stephen Fish, My Black Friend

Stephen Fish was different from the other boys in Battleview Acres for three reasons. First, he was the smartest of any of us—the oldest child of a telecommunications scientist and a straight A student. He attended brainy after-school activities like forensics and science league, while butt-heads like me broke bottles in the high school parking lot. Second, while other boys in the neighborhood played roller hockey and football, Fish ran track. Third, Fish was from the only black family in the neighborhood— a fact that we constantly said didn't matter one little bit.

Stephen and I were friends through our preteen years. He lived two blocks away, and I went over to his house a couple of afternoons a week to play Dungeons & Dragons with him and his two younger brothers. I liked the game, but when I was thirteen, the Dog convinced me that D&D—with its hardcover books and fantasy setting—was only for dorks. I remember missing D&D and the afternoons with Fish when I became too cool for him. I started playing hockey instead.

If I had any opinion about race or racism, it was shaped by the Dog's pot-enabled lectures. Using arguments made by Charles Murray and Richard Hernstein in the scandalous/scandalized *The*

Bell Curve, the Dog believed that racism largely ended in the 1960s. "The lingering 'achievement gap' between the races," the Dog once lectured, "has many reasons, but it is certainly possible that one race may be—overall—a little more or less intelligent than another." He paused for dramatic effect. "If some genetic groups are heavier, taller, less prone to certain diseases, why is it racist to think that some kinds of people are—overall—a little bit smarter or dumber? There is nothing racist about this. There are certainly very smart individuals in every race capable of 'making it'—the Fish family is clear proof of that. But there isn't," the Dog argued, "a lot of reason to give advantages to a group of people because they are—overall— less capable." In a memorable line at the end of one of his expositions on race, the Dog clinched his argument by saying, "No one ever lowered the basket for the five-feet-seven dunk-machine Spud Webb, and no one would root for him if they did."

Happily, race and racism—at least as we understood it at the time—were not issues in Morganville. In a junior year class with nearly 500 students, there were only three African-Americans— George Johnson, Sherice Thaxton, and Fish. George Johnson posed an interesting case. He lived on Wickatunk Road, in the most redneck area in the school district. Like other kids from that neighborhood, George dressed Lynard Skynard-style—ripped denim papered over with patches advertising auto and smoke-less tobacco brands. He briefly donned a denim jacket with a Confederate flag. I assume someone told George about his ward-robe malfunction because the "Stars and Bars" flag patch was soon removed. But the presence of that patch on George's jacket, even if only for a fleeting moment, says something about racial aware-ness in Morganville in the 1980s. The town was dominated by liberal ex-patriots from New York who wore their "color blind-ness" as a badge of honor. No one, not even the rednecks, gave the three African-American students a bad time. Everyone believed that racism—at least the obvious kind everyone would recognize as racism—was un-cool and ignorant.

However, there were occasions growing up when I overheard undisguised racist remarks. This was common when hanging out at parties with kids from the blue-collar towns that bordered Morganville. On such occasions, my friends and I tried to silence it. The Dog's exchange with a Carver at a party in Hazlet is one example. We called all racists "Carver" in honor of Howard Stern's running put-downs of Daniel Carver, a KKK officer who did regular guest spots on the show. The Carver was blaming n*ggers for the theft of his father's lawn furniture, when the Dog engaged him. "Excuse me, Mr. Carver, I don't want to give offense, but please understand that I find your language hurtful as my mother is Afro-American." The Carver, not sure if his leg was being pulled and not sure what to do if it was, went quiet. An hour later, the Dog, Carver, and I were chugging beers together and bonding in our common hatred of the Philadelphia Flyers.

By age sixteen, Stephen Fish and I were distant, but I always felt guilty about walking away from his friendship. On a whim, I called Fish one evening and invited him to a party at McGowan's scheduled for that Friday night. McGowan's folks were out of town, and we raised enough money for a half-keg and a six-foot sub from Dusal's. After a long pause, he said, "Yes, I'll come."

Fish showed up early, before eight, while McGowan, Kevin, and I were still prepping the house for the party. The Dog was in the backyard, supposedly setting up folding chairs, but mostly just avoiding work. For a few minutes, Fish helped me take the Saran wrap off the sub before settling on the living room couch with a cup of soda. When one of us shouted for an update on the Ranger-Penguins game that was on the TV, he shouted back "Rangers are still up 1–0," and gave no additional information. Knowing he was hockey-challenged, we accepted the minimalist updates without protest.

By ten o'clock, there were about thirty people in McGowan's house—mostly our hockey friends from both Morganville and St. Joe high schools. The beer was cold and Tony Cioffi from St. Joe's came with a fat bag of pot and a giant bong. The Rangers beat the Pens 3–0, and *Hockey Fights Volume II*—which included the cherished clip of Jimmy Mann knocking out the hated Paul Baxter—was playing through the VCR in the basement. All was right in the world.

I settled in with Kevin in the basement playing beer-pong with two girls from St. Joe's. Kevin landed a ball in my cup, so I had to chug my beer. Nearing the keg, I overheard a comment about "the black guy by himself upstairs." I bolted up the stairs two steps at a time with my cup still empty.

Fish was alone in the living room, slouched on the sofa with a cup of soda. When he saw me, he leaned forward and feigned interest in the Rangers' post-game show on TV. I asked, "Hey, why don't you come with me and get a beer and hunk of sandwich?"

"I have a track meet in the morning at eight, and need to watch what I put in my body." Then, unable to conceal some sarcasm, he continued, "Though I am having a *great time*."

But he stood up when I asked, "Will you at least keep me company on my lonely trip to the keg?"

Tony Cioffi was at the keg. He was a big guy—a football lineman who made varsity as a sophomore. On hockey skates, Tony was slow and a liability to his team, but he delivered thundering checks on the unwary—so his modest hockey accomplishments were glorified in post-game mythmaking.

At the keg, Tony poured me a beer, then he turned to Fish, "You look very thirsty, how about a cold one?"

Fish said, "No thanks." Tony made a gesture of shock and I laughed. Fish forced a smile.

Tony told me about the roller hockey team my team was playing on Sunday afternoon. "They're like bees, McDuff, so you have to skate hard and jam them up. Watch that pretty boy, Jerry Zuccic—get inside his jersey, don't let him move." He then put me in a good-natured but unbreakable headlock and dragged me over to the bong.

At the bong, I took a hit, and then reminded Tony that I had left Fish standing at the keg. Tony looked up from packing a bowl and said, "Well, bring your black friend over." Then he added, "But I hear pot makes *them* crazy."

The four of us at the bong with Tony—McGowan, Kevin, some girl whose name I can't remember, and I—went silent. Tony looked at us, and then he looked over at Fish—who stood open-mouthed fifteen feet away. Tony's face reddened. He stared down at his Nike sneakers and nervously picked at the leather Swoosh that was beginning to fall off his right shoe.

I walked over to Fish, but didn't say anything. He told me, "It's almost eleven, I have to go." I walked him out of the house. If I said anything to him as we walked, I can't remember it.

When I came back inside, McGowan and Kevin were scolding Tony. I heard the normally mellow McGowan call Tony "stupid." The Dog, not even at the bong when the comment was made, joined the hectoring. Trying to sound like the Kingfish from *Amos 'n' Andy*, the Dog called out to me as I returned to the room, "Hey McDuff, which of his kinfolk does Tony resemble more, his pappy Jimmy "the Greek" or his mammy Al Campanis?[1] Tony will be visiting them this weekend at the Old Carvers' retirement home."

Tony kept repeating "my screw-up" and "really sorry" after each remark, and kept picking at the Swoosh on his sneaker. Unlike my friends, I felt no need to scold Tony—I knew he was going to beat himself up for weeks about this. Despite his jumbo frame, Tony disappeared unnoticed from the party sometime before midnight. His pot, bong, and the Swoosh from his sneaker—now completely torn off—were left behind.

Fish and I had already drifted out of our friendship before the party, so neither of us lost anything tangible that night. He was in advanced placement courses and academic-achiever after-school activities, so I rarely saw him in school. When we met, there was always a smile and friendly wave—but that was it.

---

1. Jimmy "the Greek" Snyder was a famous gambler and sports prognosticator. His TV career abruptly ended after his remark that black athletes were successful because they "were bred for sports" during slavery. Al Campanis was a senior executive for the Los Angeles Dodgers until he commented "that most blacks don't have the faculties" to become baseball managers.

Fɪsʜ ᴀɴᴅ I crossed paths again seven years later. I was finishing up grad school and selling cars at the Honda dealer in Freehold part-time. (I hated selling cars and was lousy at it.) He was a new-lywed who had just purchased a house in Freehold. He came in to buy an Accord, and after a test drive, bought the car from me without haggling. Making small talk while doing the paperwork with him after the sale, I chattered a bit about some of the people from high school we both knew. I mentioned that I was still close to McGowan, Kevin Kopf, and Lynette Robson, and gossiped a bit about them.

Fish gave me a serious look, "Hey, McDuff, I am really sad about what happened to the Dog. Sorry that I never reached out to you."

I said, "That's okay. Do you have any dirt on anyone from Morganville High School?"

"You know, I just have not made enough of an effort to keep in touch. I've only kept up with a couple."

"Well, who are these lucky people?" I asked, not understanding his reluctance.

He looked away and said, "I'm only in contact with two: George Johnson and Sherice Thaxton."

It troubles me to this day that the three African-American stu-dents from my graduating class self-segregated after graduation. While drafting this story, I called Fish and invited myself over to his house in hopes of talking with him about race. Fish's appre-hension was palpable over the phone, and he said he was busy on the first date I proposed. So I said, "You name any day this year, and I will be there. I really want to do this. It will be fun, honest." He acquiesced.

We had a nice dinner. His wife is a beautiful, elegant African woman who grew up in Ghana. She speaks with perfect British diction and her knowledge of the Anglo literary canon shames mine. They have four children—each one sharp as a tack and well-mannered.

Fish was a gracious host, but he evaded questions about his "racial experience" in Morganville, other than acknowledging that

that he was aware of his differentness all through his childhood. I left his house that evening disappointed.

A week later I received a book in the mail from Amazon.com, *The Rage of a Privileged Class: Why Are Middle-Class Blacks Angry? Why Should America Care?* by Ellis Cose. In three starts at the book, I have not made it past page fifty.

DISCUSSION WITH LISA:

I walked into Lisa's office feeling good. Since the story was about the least black African-American I had ever met, I decided to do an exaggerated Hip-Hop Star walk heading to the rocking chair. I called, "Yo-Yo-Yo to my home girl, Moscovitz. Da' Bully is in the House!"

Lisa made a pained expression.

"You didn't like this week's episode of *Homicide: Life on the Streets of Morganville*?" I became a little more serious, "No shit. What did you think about this story? I went into some new territory this week."

Lisa looked in the air. "Well, I think this is an interesting story from a sociological perspective— a nuanced discussion about race in a suburb that hoped it was post-racial. But I wonder what you were trying to show me in this story?"

"I guess I'm trying to show you that I walked away from a budding friendship with a nice guy because he was nerdy and different—not because he was black."

"So, you wrote this to absolve yourself of the stain of racism. Was this ever in doubt?"

"I don't know. You're the headshrinker, you tell me." I hated the way I sounded, but it was too late—the words were out.

"Okay then, Matthew. What I think is that you probably are racist on some level, or at least worry that you might be. Maybe you used this story to tell me and, more importantly, tell yourself that you are not. What do you think?"

My cheeks flushed at the statement. "That's nice. So you think my 'nuanced story on race' is a lie?"

"Not necessarily, but I question if you cherry-picked a set of facts that allows you to paint yourself as better than you might have been." She shifted in her chair. "Let me take a different tack. In your story, it appears that you are Stephen's friend, the only boy in the neighborhood who plays nerdy games with him, invites him to parties, etc. So why was he unhappy to hear from you years later?"

Her question made me uncomfortable. I thought about leaving or telling her to buzz off. But Lisa waited, her eyes fixed on mine. I squirmed in my seat.

Finally, I came clean. "Fine. Fish was not crazy about hearing from me because there were moments when I was every bit as ignorant as Tony Cioffi. The story I wrote is true, but I selected the moments with Fish that would let me look okay. Fish didn't want to hear from me because he probably thinks I am a jerk, though a well-intentioned jerk." I felt no relief from making this statement. I was disgusted with myself—and disgusted with Lisa for making me own up to this.

"How is this supposed to be helping me?" I asked angrily.

"There's no assurance that you will feel good about every moment of every session. Therapy doesn't work that way. But uncomfortable moments can be helpful too."

"I know that. Can I leave early today?"

"You can always leave early. This is not high school, and I am not your clock-watching teacher."

"Can I stop writing stories for you?"

"Yes, you can stop writing these stories, but you need to ask yourself what happens if you do. I didn't think we were doing well together before we had your stories as a touchstone to stimulate meaningful discussion. As you have told me, these stories are a mechanism for reliving episodes in your life that you were unable to explore until now. Just be aware of what we—what you—lose if you stop writing them."

Without saying anything, I stood up and left the room—twenty minutes before the session usually ended. Leaving early was an empty, immature gesture. We both knew it. There was no doubt in my mind I would write another story. Heck, I had already settled on the next topic even before the session about Fish: I would tell Lisa about the guy who could have, even should have, been a great friend—if not for the Dog.

9

Barry Big-Hair

On the first day of school of my junior year, an unfamiliar boy entered my homeroom. My eyes were pulled to him by his Afro, big nose, and the early attempts at a beard. He wore a tie-dye shirt, with a cartoon skeleton on the front, a symbol of the Grateful Dead.

"Woodstock's up the road a-ways from here, Mr. Groovy," I sassed as he walked by me and slouched into an open seat. In Morganville High School, where boys dressed like Don Johnson from *Miami Vice* and girls like Madonna, Barry Rubin was an odd sight to behold. For months, heads turned when he walked down the hall.

The Dog, Kevin, McGowan, and I considered the Grateful Dead's music atonal and boring. However, we liked Deadheads, because, as the Dog once said, "They don't care about being mocked and they share their pot." Barry did not disappoint in either regard; he was a great sport about the shots we took at him, and happily hosted pot-smoking sessions in his car before gym.

Barry moved to New Jersey from Vermont when his college professor father took a faculty appointment at Rutgers. He came with a Vermont driver's license. This made Barry a valuable after-school chauffeur as the Dog and I counted down the days to our driving tests. Barry drove a rusted-out '75 Nova with no A/C or FM radio; water seeped in through the windows when it rained.

Still, his car was a great hangout. The Dog lovingly named it "Dukakis's Eyebrows on wheels" before his relationship with Barry went south. Lacking FM radio, we became fans of Howard Stern in the mornings and sports talk radio in the afternoons. The final demise of the car came when heavyset McGowan put his foot through the bottom of the car and burned his leg on the catalytic converter. After that, the car was junked for $100.

———

I LOVED that Barry took on the Dog in contests of stupid TV trivia—a field of study on which the Dog had proclaimed himself "omniscient." The Dog once asked a question about a *Bewitched* episode. "What was Sabrina's (Samantha's mischievous cousin also played by Elizabeth Montgomery) nickname for Larry Tate (Darrin's obsequious boss)?" Barry quickly answered, "Cotton Top." The Dog went pale.

Since the Dog was previously regarded as invincible on all kinds of worthless knowledge, Kevin offered cheers and toasts to "Barry, the Great" and "Barry, the Brave." Then I offered a toast: "Barry, Toppler of Trivia Tyrants," and finally, "Barry, Slayer of Know-It-Alls." The Dog scowled.

Later that week, the Dog started making fun of Barry's long nose, calling him "Rose-Nose" when a big zit grew on it. The abu-sive nicknames progressed to "Nostrilla" after Barry confessed to never having watched a Godzilla movie, and "Nostrildamus" after Barry successfully predicted the huge commercial success of Huey Lewis's jock-rock album, *Sports*. One day in the school cafeteria, Barry finally pushed back: "Man, Dog, it ain't funny anymore, and besides, your nose is way bigger than mine."

This led to a very public bet in which I was selected to measure whose nose was bigger. A master gossip, Kevin seized upon the opportunity to take sides, take bets, and make a spectacle of the disagreement. Soon $380 was drummed-up in wagers from twenty or so knuckleheads with nothing better to do—including forty dol-lars of Kevin's own money on Barry having the bigger nose.

As the crowd of bettors gathered after school behind the cafeteria, Barry and the Dog argued about the best way to measure nose size. With my mediation, they agreed on my proposal "to measure from the top of the nose to where it merged into the upper jaw." Using a six-inch ruler on the flat side of a protractor, I conducted the initial measuring. When I announced to the crowd, "The Dog's nose measures one-sixteenth of an inch longer than Barry's," the Dog went nuts. "This is bullshit. All we've proven is Big-Hair has an ape's jutting jaw. The only appropriate measure of the bigger nose is to measure mass—it needs to be a water displacement test."

I looked at Barry; he nodded his assent. I called "Game on!" Kevin started taking bets again.

The water displacement test proved impossible to administer fairly as both contestants, but particularly the Dog, accused the other of not sticking his entire nose into the water-filled beaker I lifted from the Chemistry lab. And so the contest to measure the bigger nose ended in confusion and accusations. But the Dog relented on the big-nose insults due to the established certainty that his nose was at least approximately as large as Barry's.

—◦—

ALTHOUGH HE was from Vermont, Barry didn't ice skate and in his own words, "never played a lot of sports." But Kevin and I liked him, so we recruited him to play hockey with us. He sucked, so we made him a permanent goalie. With repetition, Barry became tolerably good at it.

The Dog, however, was always skeptical about the efforts to bring Barry into our clique. He sometimes called Barry "Yoko," implying that Barry was a disruptive influence on Morganville's Fab Four. Most of the time, however, the Dog called Barry "Big-Hair," though we frowned at him when he did.

The spring-summer hockey league at Freedom Tree Park started in April. My team—with the Dog, Kevin, and McGowan and me at the core—was below average. But we were optimistic going into the season because McGowan had recruited two talented players from St. Joe's to play with us, the non-identical twins, Gregory and Joseph Barilkus. We dubbed them "the Russians" because they circled behind each other for drop-passes, a tactic unique to the Eastern Bloc hockey players first speckling NHL team rosters in the 1980s. We later learned that as ethnic Lithuanians, the Barilkus brothers hated being called "Russians." They left us for another team the following year. But that season, the Barilkus boys gave our team two gifted scorers. The other cause for optimism—or so we told ourselves—was the presence of our first full-time goalie, Barry.

Our first game was against a team of ice hockey players from Old Bridge. The Old Bridge boys took high-torque slap shots that made the ball whistle as it spun through the air. We never beat the Old Bridge teams, but by stepping on sticks, grabbing jerseys, elbowing, etc., we kept most games close. The problem was we never mounted much offense. The Russian brothers changed that by scoring five goals between them. We headed into the game's last two minutes tied 6–6.

Then Barry let in a terribly soft goal on a shot taken from well outside the blue line. The Dog went crazy, shouting, "That big-haired, big-nosed shithead lost us the game!" He started throwing equipment onto the rink. The Dog received a penalty for the ruckus. The Old Bridge team scored again on the power play, and we lost 8–6.

Driving home from the game with me, the Dog continued his anti-Barry tirade, telling me, "I don't understand why we are nice to Big-Hair. He sucks at hockey and I can get us pot anytime. You and Kevin are driving, we don't need him. Cut him loose." There was no talking to the Dog when he was on a bender, so I let him go on without saying anything.

The following Monday, the Dog skipped the pot-smoking session in Barry's car.

Our next after-school hockey game was Tuesday. There were only eight players, which meant no goalies, and everyone skated. Barry and Shawn Miers (three years younger and just a beginner) were split up because any team with both of them would surely lose.

About a half-hour into the game, Barry went against the boards for a loose ball. The Dog ran at him at full speed and leaped so that the Dog's elbow met Barry's head. Barry's head slammed against the chain-linked fence boards with such force that Barry landed headfirst on the concrete floor.

For maybe twenty seconds, Barry did not move. A small pool of blood formed on the floor around his head and he started groaning. Kevin and I picked him up and rushed him to Freehold Hospital where he was admitted with a concussion and skull laceration requiring nine stitches. Most of us played without helmets, but Barry and two other beginners wore helmets and pads. We called them "powder puffs" for wearing the protective gear. The doctor who attended to Barry that afternoon said, "That helmet saved your friend from a life-threatening skull fracture."

This savage incident was the final blow to our three-year run of after-school pick-up hockey. After it, some parents banned their sons from playing with us. Other boys, fearing us, claimed their parents banned them too. We never again reached the necessary eight-person quorum needed for even a lame after-school game.

———◆———

Barry and I remained friendly after the incident, and I continued to smoke pot with him. But when I did, I chose not to mention it to my other friends.

After high school, Barry went to Rutgers, graduated with honors, and then stayed on to earn a Masters degree in Food Science. He was the subject of a feature article in the New Brunswick *Home News* for developing a new kind of artificial raspberry flavoring while a grad student. I continued to meet him for drinks and dinner a couple of times a year at Doll's Place, a mom and pop pub with homemade lasagna and Guinness on tap (a rarity at the time). We stayed in touch into our mid-twenties, then life got in the way and we drifted apart. I lost contact with him for about ten years.

Barry and I met again a few years ago. His wife and my wife share a common acquaintance, and the three women gleefully arranged the meeting of us long-lost friends. We met at Barry's favorite Portuguese restaurant in Newark. He ordered for me that night—shrimp in garlic sauce, pan-seared asparagus, and a thin steak cooked at the table on a clay tile heated by a Bunsen burner. It was one of the best dinners of my life.

Barry lives with his wife (no children) in a hip area of Hoboken, just across from Manhattan. He reverse-commutes away from New York City each day, working in the labs of a giant pharmaceutical company near New Brunswick. He heads up a R&D team responsible for developing "gradual release dissolvable delivery systems." To lay people, this means he develops new and improved capsules and pill coatings. He still smokes pot on weekends and special occasions. As we finished dinner, he offered. I declined.

DISCUSSION WITH LISA:

I came into Lisa's office hoping that the unpleasantness of the previous week was past.

She offered up an olive branch as I entered. "Hey, I know last week was difficult for you, but I want you to know that I think we're making good progress together and I think that your stories have been critical in that regard."

I smiled, but didn't want to rehash the previous week. "Yes. I think the stories are helping me. But I want to talk about Barry Big-Hair?"

"Okay. How is this story different from your story about Stephen Fish?"

"Well, I picked a story that really reminds me what a piece of shit the Dog was. I was not the piece of shit, he was. Barry was, still is, a really good guy. He could have been my best friend in high school had I met him before the Dog. I would have fallen in with the smart crowd, and still smoked dope. Win-win. He should have been my best friend, not the Dog, but that never happened. The Dog, the jealous little shit, would never have allowed it. I have never really had a 'best friend' since." I was surprised by my bluntness, but it was true.

Lisa waited before speaking, as if to reassure me that she understood the importance of what I'd just said. "What about your other friends, McGowan and Kevin Kopf? I thought they're your oldest and best friends."

I thought about why I had never considered either McGowan or Kevin my *best* friend. I didn't know what I wanted to say, but the words came out anyway. "Well, don't get me wrong, McGowan and Kevin are both great friends. I would do anything for either of them. But there's a special role for your *best* friend. This is the person who knows what you are thinking without dialogue. McGowan and Kevin make me laugh like no one else can. They have both saved my ass, and either would happily do so again. But they don't totally get me."

"Couldn't Diane be your best friend?"

"God, no," I chuckled.

"What about Lynette—could she be your best friend?"

I thought about this, "Maybe, but we see each other too infrequently—due to distance and the discomfort it causes our spouses. And I'm not sure I could have a woman as my best friend—it's just not in the cards."

"Your story about Barry and this conversation reinforces what you've told me previously about your relationship with the Dog, but only adds to my sense that I do not understand your feelings toward your old high school friends. I mean the living ones, of course, McGowan and Kevin Kopf. Would you want to tell me about them?"

I was surprised by Lisa's caution. "Sure, Lisa, but why do you have to ask me like that? Just tell me you want me to write about McGowan and Kevin next."

"If I was a little cautious in making this request, it's because the first time I asked you to tell me about your friends [she looked at her notes] was when we were discussing Rocco, your hockey rival. At that time, you responded rather distrustfully. I take it as a good sign that you're ready to move to the most important people in your life."

I let her have the last word without further comment.

10

McGowan

Patrick McGowan grew up a block away from me. I started playing with him when I was six, but because he went to the Catholic schools, I didn't see him all that much. McGowan was a tall boy with a heavy frame. Between growth spurts, he'd get fat. Dinner at the McGowan's house always included large portions red meat, and usually mashed potatoes. Ice cream on a stick was the after-school snack and ice cream in a bowl was the nightly dessert. When I was a teenager, my parents dined out without me. Usually, they left me ten dollars for pizza or Chinese takeout; I pocketed the money and ate with the McGowans. This pleased me almost as much as it pleased the hospitable Mrs. McGowan.

McGowan took up hockey two years after the Dog and me, and a year after Kevin, but he was the star of our team and one of the best defensemen in the league. Blessed with a wingspan to match his six-foot-three frame, no forward could get around him with the ball. The better skaters tried beating him by playing "dump and chase" (whacking the ball into the corner and then racing for it), but the deceptively fast McGowan always picked up the ball first. Despite his girth, McGowan didn't go headhunting opponents like the rest of us. When he body-checked, he only pushed his opponent off the ball, while the rest of us aimed for spectacular body-checks designed to hurt or at least humiliate opponents.

McGowan loved professional wrestling. When adults were not around, he grabbed the closest sucker and started executing professional wrestling moves. I was on the receiving end of at least a dozen Camel Clutches—his favorite move—but also Abdominal Stretches, Sleeper Holds, and Suplexes. McGowan once performed a belly-to-belly Suplex on me that sent me flying onto his bed. The force of my landing broke the bed and pushed the bed's headboard through the bedroom wall. I was fine, but McGowan was punished: he was banned from watching wrestling for a month. But despite having a bear's body and being frequently drunk when performing his wrestling moves, no one was ever hurt. McGowan was infallibly gentle, with only one exception—which will be discussed soon enough.

What McGowan loved most about wrestling were the cartoonish personalities. He memorized favorite lines from bad-guy wrestlers and delivered them involuntarily when prompted. Whenever a football broadcaster referred to the Dallas Cowboys as "America's Team," McGowan shouted, in the voice of the anti-American villain, the Iron Sheik, "Iran number one, U.S.A. ah-tuh" (with a phlegm spit onto the ground). When anything resembling the Russian language was heard, he'd announce, "Please rise and respect Mr. Volkoff's singing of the Soviet national anthem." Then he'd start singing the first few lines of the Soviet National Anthem in the voice of Cold War bad guy, Nikolai Volkoff.

But most of all, McGowan loved Rowdy Roddy Piper's hot-cold malevolence. Any reference to the Pacific Islands forced McGowan into Piper's monologue against Pacific Islander good guy, Jimmy Snuka. This climaxed with McGowan shouting, "Well, have a coconut, Jungle Man," and smashing an imaginary coconut across the head of the closest person. (There are clips of all of these wrestlers and the Piper-Snuka incident on YouTube.)

McGowan's obsession with professional wrestling twisted his artistic gift. As a boy, he played piano and made lovely drawings of backyards, sporting events, and family scenes. I remember my mother telling me, "Patrick is so polite, and his pictures make his parents so happy. You should be more like him." By high school,

McGowan was still drawing, but only the heads of professional wrestlers.

He stated, with great seriousness, "Wrestlers have the most expressive faces in the world." On an outsized sketch pad, McGowan drew pencil sketches of the older wrestlers like Greg "The Hammer" Valentine, George "The Animal" Steele, and Don "The Magnificent" Muraco—the last men standing from the era when wrestlers executed their craft nightly in small-town high school gymnasiums. McGowan's drawings depicted wrestlers straining or in agony— they were often being choked—and the scars on their faces were more prominent than in real life. Yet the drawings were almost photographic in their precision. The Dog called McGowan the John Singleton Copley of pro-wrestling.

———

McGowan happily brought the Dog and me with him to St. Joe's parties. St. Joe's was a sociologically odd school because it drew students from all over Monmouth County, from working class to wealthy. Once, McGowan took us to a party at a swanky house in Holmdel with an inground pool and basketball court. A party tent was stretched over the basketball court with a half-dozen tables, forty chairs, and catered fried chicken and burgers. Not knowing what we were getting into, we showed up without bathing suits, and our cutoff shorts and T-shirts contrasted mightily with the preppy boys' Docker shorts and upturned collar golf shirts. But McGowan was a cult hero to the host—perfectly named Avery Swain—and settled in entertaining a small crowd with his pro-wrestling moves and impersonations.

The Dog and I were bored, so we grabbed up the ketchup packets from the catering table, dropped them on the ground, and started splattering the ketchup by stepping on them. Soon we were competing to see who could squirt ketchup farther. We grabbed a dozen packets each and exploded ketchup all across the party tent, not caring that we were getting it all over the personal effects of the partygoers.

A girl with a squeaky voice and a newly red-striped leather bag forced her boyfriend's attention, and he swaggered over to us with two preppy jock friends in tow. After exchanging some pleasantries, the Dog was pinned to the ground by the boyfriend and I was in a pre-fight chest-to-chest ritual with a thick-armed preppy who, assuming he knew how to fight, would certainly kick my ass. The third preppy stood by, ready to assist.

McGowan came running into the mix. He pushed the third preppy hard, sending him flying out of the tent. In the same motion, he doubled-over the guy who had pinned the Dog with a kick to the midsection. Then he wheeled around the guy who was chest-to-chest with me and punched him in the cheek. Apparently this first blow was just for measurement. An instant later, a second thundering plow landed on the same cheek.

We heard the cheekbone crack as the preppy fell to the ground. McGowan looked at his hand, stunned—like Michael Corleone in *The Godfather* after blowing away Virgil "The Turk" Solozzo. McGowan and I stood next to each other over the fallen guy. It all happened too quickly for the preppies—or anyone else—to react. The Dog, using a voice borrowed from Shaggy in the Scooby-Doo cartoons, called out "Zoiks! Let's get out of here." It snapped me and McGowan back to reality. Soon we were running for McGowan's car.

The shock of breaking a guy's face lifted quickly for the Dog and me. On the ride home, I asked the Dog, "Which sound was loudest: the *thwack* of McGowan's fist hitting cheek, the *thud* of that guy hitting the ground, or the *crunch* of the bone giving way?" The Dog replied, "I think the proper order is thwack, crunch, thud. But the thud of that guy's body hitting the cement was certainly the loudest. It had the impact of an earth tremor." Then we started imitating the sounds in sequence. McGowan fought back tears.

To honor McGowan and snap him out of the pussy behavior, the Dog started discussing the incident in the context of a recent professional wrestling melodrama. He said, "You know, our scrap with those preppies was like when André the Giant [McGowan] rescued Chief Jay and Jules Strongbow [the Dog and me] from that unfair match against the three Wild Samoans [the preppies]. The riled-up Giant cleaned house on all three Samoans without assistance." I joined in by chanting "André, André" from the backseat.

Though silent, McGowan started smiling at the fictionalized, pro wrestling-inflected version of the event. Subsequent retellings of the story were interspersed with pro-wrestling moves and tag lines that never really happened but made for better copy. McGowan's retellings, however, never mentioned his post-event sadness. Out of respect to him, I never mentioned that element of the story either—until now.

WHEN HE and I were twenty-two, McGowan started seeing a twenty-eight-year-old former go-go dancer from Keansburg—the toughest white town in Monmouth County. The woman, Angela something, left go-go dancing not because of any newfound virtue, but because she had grown too tubby for the profession. McGowan got her pregnant and, as a good Catholic boy must, proposed marriage. To everyone's profound disappointment, she accepted.

Standing on the balcony of a room at the Thunderbird Motel in Wildwood at four AM after his bachelor party, I asked McGowan, "How's Angela going to be as the mother of your baby?" McGowan grabbed me by the shirt, pulled me close and whispered, "Angela's a turd." They married the next day.

THE MCGOWAN family lived with his parents for about five years. Then, about fifteen years ago, Angela split and never came back. Adriana McGowan is now nineteen. McGowan and McGowan's mom raised her great. She's a confident young woman who has won many awards for her piano compositions. Adriana's a freshman with a generous scholarship/financial aid package from

Albright College, a good liberal arts school an hour west of Philly. She jams in a band led by a pair of self-consciously fat, rich kids, The Corpulent Plutocrats.

I am Adriana's godfather and I continue to do what I can for her. This includes taking her to a concert or an opera annually at one of New York City's elite musical venues. Last year it was the Kronos Quartet—which I enjoyed for about twenty minutes. Most years, we take in an opera at the Met which I will finally admit to enjoying. Adrianna repeats the line she once heard from me, "Opera: It's better than you think. It has to be." She still calls me "uncle."

For my most recent birthday, Adriana gave me a framed sketch that her father drew in high school. It is a pencil drawing of the head and shoulders of the wrestler Greg Valentine. His face is full of anguish as he struggles to free himself from the choke hold of an opponent with incredibly large hands (probably André the Giant). Valentine's face is putty and sweaty, but his most prominent facial feature is a series of vertical scars on his forehead—places where he cut himself as part of the script from earlier matches. It hangs over my bedroom dresser and I love it every bit as much as Diane hates it.

McGowan never remarried and still lives in his parents' house, now caring for his declining mother. Before that, McGowan helped his obese father through several years of worsening diabetes that included the amputation of a leg. The diabetes led to heart problems that killed Mr. McGowan at age sixty-eight. Despite caring for one sick parent or the other almost continuously for seven years and being a single parent to boot, McGowan never complains about his tough domestic situation. Except for the month that his father was in hospice, McGowan's never had any respite longer than the weekend-long parent-sitting by his older sister. When I comment on his admirable fortitude as a caregiver, he jokingly calls himself "just another Irish mother" and changes the subject.

McGowan works for the State of New Jersey in some kind of regulatory position that involves overseeing the state's utilities. He once explained to me that he audits them to ensure their compliance with various New Jersey laws; but since he's not a finance guy, I don't exactly know what that means.

McGowan never talks about his job except to complain about pervasive slackness in the state's workforce. "Seeing state government in action," he says, "has made me a 'ditto-head'"—a term used by Rush Limbaugh listeners to identify each other. Right-wing talk radio is nearly always on in the McGowan house.

I frequently kid McGowan about his devotion to his "Maha Rushi." This includes gleefully reminding him about the overly colorful off-air life of his radio hero. Six months ago at one-thirty in the morning, on beer number eight, I went on an anti-Limbaugh bender: "Your hero, the man who ties half his brain behind his back to make it a fair fight, has been arrested for possessing mountains of prescription drugs, done a stint in drug rehab, failed as a late-night TV personality, failed as a sports commentator, married and divorced something like five times, and was told 'no thanks' by the NFL when he tried to buy a football team. How can you believe in this guy?"

McGowan shrugged it off, "And Jefferson slept with his slaves, but the Declaration of Independence still turned out okay."

At my request, Adrianna resets her father's programmed car radio stations to National Public Radio and alternative rock whenever she's home from college. It's a running joke among the three of us.

McGowan and I go out for a beer whenever I am in Morganville visiting Dad. Until a few years ago, McGowan and I met for one or two New Jersey Devils hockey games a year. But he's very heavy and, although he won't admit it, I think standard-size arena seats are difficult for him.

I have long tweaked McGowan about his weight, which included running an annual New Year's Eve pool where participants threw in twenty dollars to guess his weight. But I stopped three years ago when McGowan asked me to cut it out. I now only ask him about his weight privately and with the seriousness of an old friend who really cares about him. The last time McGowan gave up a specific figure, he admitted to weighing 295—which I suspect is an understatement.

A month ago, McGowan told me he needed to see a doctor because of bladder problems. He sent me an email the next day, "The doc ran some tests. It's now official, I have diabetes."

Discussion with Lisa:

As I settled in my chair, Lisa asked, "You really like McGowan, don't you?"

"I would do anything for him. He is a good friend, and probably the nicest guy I've ever known."

"Your words about McGowan touched me." I heard a little tightness in her voice. "Your other stories were not like this one— so sad and sympathetic."

I was floored. I said "thanks" and stopped, not sure what else to say—but knowing I should say more. There was a long silence.

"What would McGowan say if he read this story?" Lisa finally asked.

"It depends. He's a positive and friendly guy on the surface, but he's private and very sensitive underneath. If I gave the story to him and he knew it was only for him, I think he'd be good with it; he might even like the story. But if it was a public document, I think he'd kick my ass. No one wants their life's worst moments read by the town crier."

Then we digressed briefly to the phenomenon of reality TV and the way contestants revel in being publicly embarrassed each week. So I qualified my earlier statement. "Well, people like McGowan don't want their dirty underwear exposed."

"Why didn't you tell me about McGowan's relationship with the Dog? I know more about McGowan's relationship with André the Giant than the Dog."

This was a good question and one that I had not considered. "Well, McGowan's a special guy in that he never had problems with anyone growing up. He was always the 'jolly fat guy.' The Dog pissed off everyone at least once, everyone except McGowan. Of the four of us—the Dog, Kevin, McGowan, and me—McGowan was and is the only gentleman in the bunch."

Lisa nodded, "Is it possible that you chose not to note McGowan's easy relationship with the Dog because it goes against the picture of the Dog you are painting—the Dog as an asshole who got what he deserved?"

I didn't like the question, but fought off the urge to respond defensively. "There's probably some truth to that."

We talked for another fifteen minutes, but I was already onto the next story. Now that I had discussed McGowan, it was time to move into more dangerous territory. It was time to write about Kevin Kopf.

11

Kevin Kopf

W hen Kevin was just seven, his father split. Poppa Kopf left
for Florida with a sexy woman half his age. She tended
the little bar at the Arnold Palmer Driving Range that Poppa Kopf
frequented. After that, Kevin's mom couldn't hold things together. I
remember her sobbing for hours over coffee by day and wine by
night with my mom, and overhearing conversations between my
parents in which my mom always said something like, "I need
to stop sitting around with Janet. It's no good for either of us." I
remember my parents whispering the word "alcoholic," thinking I
would not overhear or understand.

One night, while Kevin was sleeping over at my house, the
Kopf house caught on fire with Mrs. Kopf inside. The fire was
extinguished and only two rooms—including the master bedroom
where Mrs. Kopf slept—were seriously damaged. Stories of an
attempted suicide-by-arson spread throughout the neighborhood.
Mrs. Kopf went away to a place my older brothers sensitively
termed "the loony bin." My father joked, "Janet's on vacation at
the Hotel Silly."

While I was in kindergarten, a social worker took Kevin out
of his first grade class and shipped him to Florida. That afternoon
my mother told me, "Matty, Kevin has gone to Florida to live with
his father. Please don't be too sad about this." I ran across the
street and started hurling rocks at Mrs. Kopf's car. I remember

punching at my older brothers as they tried to corral me. My father consoled me with characteristic sensitivity, "These things happen sometimes, but you'll get over it. Stop carrying on—you're not a baby anymore."

After several months, the Kopf house was repaired. Mrs. Kopf returned home; her mother came to live with her. Mrs. Kopf was very kind to me and the other neighborhood boys, and brought us little treats when she saw us playing outside. Each time she told us, "Kevin is coming home to stay next Christmas"—though several Christmases passed without his return. My parents counseled me with great gravity, "Always be polite to Janet Kopf, but never go into *that* house."

When I was thirteen, Kevin came home. His father was in jail following a Jerry Springeresque episode involving Kevin's stepmom, a younger guy without pants on, and a baseball bat upside the guy's head. Kevin tells me he has a Daytona Beach *Post* article on the incident, but I've never seen it. The stepmom divorced Mr. Kopf while he wasted two years in jail, and a family court made Mrs. Kopf Kevin's custodial parent again. As the stepmom never adopted Kevin while married to Mr. Kopf, she had no basis for challenging Mrs. Kopf for custody of Kevin. There is no evidence to suggest that the stepmom ever tried.

———

NOBODY EVER asked Kevin about his difficult family life. Kevin, however, brought it up when convenient, especially when seeking sympathy from cute girls. Unlike the Dog and me, whose quirkiness turned off most girls, and McGowan, who was shy and heavy, Kevin was cute and clever. He fed girls lines like, "Because of my hard upbringing—Dad spent time in jail, Mom spent time in a psych hospital—I can really appreciate your beauty and sincerity. I don't think I have ever met anyone quite like you." The girl of the week bought it every time.

Kevin fooled around a lot, but never had a steady girlfriend in high school. In his own words, he "burned through" women and remained friends with none of them afterward. So he relied on a network of cheese-balls and pretty-boys to constantly introduce him to new girls.

Most weekends I saw Kevin only on Friday nights; he'd go out with a carload of girls on Saturday. At times, this complicated his relationship with me, but I never pushed him too hard. Kevin kept a sense of humor about his womanizing that reminded me, the Dog, and McGowan that "the boys" always came first, even when he was ditching us on Saturday nights for (to use his phrase) "a chance to get my dick wet."

Kevin had—still has—a sick sense of humor, but also a strong sense of honor. For example, when discussing the Dog's blossoming fourteen-year-old sister, Rachel, Kevin joked, "If there's grass on the field, play ball!" But when Rachel attempted to flirt with Kevin, he abruptly cut it off by telling her, "Rach, you have a smoking little bod, but you're too young. Talk to me when you're sixteen."

He was like that about other things too. He'd tell jokes about the Ethiopian famine: What do you call an Ethiopian with a dime on his head? Answer: a nail. What's the difference between an Ethiopian toddler and a NFL football? Answer: The football must weigh at least twenty-two ounces. But Kevin was the only teen in the neighborhood who went door to door for Oxfam, the famine relief charity.

Kevin insisted, "I only volunteer for charities to meet women." But he was—and is—tremendously generous with his time and money. In a medieval Catholic way, Kevin is saving his soul not by reducing his sins, but by countering them with an abundance of good deeds. If St. Peter or someone else up there is keeping an accurate count of his various misdeeds and mitzvahs, I bet Kevin's running an ever-so-slight balance in the good deeds column.

At seventeen, Kevin was a wiry six-footer in that small cohort of boys blessed with big biceps and shoulders without ever working out. To hustle beer money and impress girls, Kevin liked to challenge random guys at parties, "Dude, you got girl arms.

Twenty dollars says I can do twice as many push-ups as you." He rarely lost a bet.

Nearly every month, Kevin beat up someone just to, in his words, "keep the legend alive." His pre-bout wisecracks were far more memorable than the lopsided fights. Before beating the tar out of Vince Cappola, for example, he said, "I'm going to drop you like a prom dress." Before ruining the face of Franky Cardinal, Kevin taunted, "I'm going to rip off your head and shit down your throat." I considered Kevin's tough-guy lines the apex of humor.

Kevin was the number two ranked pugilist in my high school class; his only loss was a narrow decision on points to "Big Al" Boyce that left both boys bloodied. It is worth noting that "Big Al" backed out of a rematch saying a fight might get him thrown off the football team while he was being scouted. This was bull. He didn't want to go up against Kevin again.

By JUNIOR year, Kevin, McGowan, the Dog, and I were as tight as any four boys. Kevin gave each of us derogatory nicknames: the Dog was called "Shylock" (the scheming Jewish moneylender from Shakespeare's *Merchant of Venice*), though Kevin used more obvious anti-Semitic slurs like kike or Christ-killer when he was angry with the Dog. McGowan was alternately called "the Pillsbury Dough Boy" or "Chewbacca" (the lovable apelike brute from the *Star Wars* movies). I was usually called "McSpic" or "Sombrero," an incorrect reference to my mother's Puerto Rican bloodline. (Sombreros are Mexican hats unknown in Puerto Rico.) As the toughest boy in our clique, we all understood that Kevin was entitled to give us insulting nicknames, and the names were—in that strange male way—spoken endearingly. Kevin was conscious of when to avoid using them—we were never humiliated in front of adults or girls.

Kevin was a year older than the rest of us, but we were all juniors together. This was because Kevin *lost* a year somewhere with all the school switching between New Jersey and Florida. Nobody ever said he was left back. Because of this, Kevin was driving a year before us. He inherited his mom's old light-blue Buick.

We had amazing times in that car. To keep things "legal"— New Jersey police frowned on minors drinking heavily while driving—we kept our beers in coolers on the floor of the backseat. Beers were immediately poured into empty tinted soda bottles, and the cans were discarded in the trunk via a shoot created by pulling out one of the rear speakers. At the bottom of the shoot was a milk crate with a trash liner. This worked well, except on sharp, fast turns (Kevin took many) when the empty cans in the milk crate rolled noisily against each other. The Dog called this "the percussion section," but the noise actually sounded something like laughter. Often after telling a bad joke, Kevin jammed on the brakes to underscore his punch line with laughter from his "beer-can studio audience."

KEVIN, THE Dog and I frequently cut school together. Usually, we drove around and smoked pot until eleven when, assailed by the munchies, we appeared first on line for the lunch buffet at China Star. We paid four-fifty to eat disgusting amounts of food until the buffet closed at two. After perhaps a dozen of these gorge-fests, the restaurant owner came out, and in a stammering Chinese accent said, "I will call police for you boys. Druggies not welcome at China Star." As we hastily exited the restaurant for the last time, the Dog called the owner a "Zipper-head" and Kevin tipped over the buffet table.

We never found a comparable lunch buffet, but three-for-a-dollar éclairs at Donut Chef (when ordered before noon) were almost as good. For five dollars, we'd each order twelve éclairs and a soda. Kevin drew giggles from the cute Russian-immigrant cashier by adding, "Make sure that soda is diet; I need to maintain my girlish figure." After Kevin slept with the cashier, we never went back to Donut Chef.

ONE SUNNY day in May, we cut school to go to the beach. The colleges were out, so the Jersey shore beaches were packed. (Doubly so, as this was the era before meddlesome environmentalists riled up New Jerseyians about swimming in New York City's filth.) We drove up and down Shore Avenue in Belmar looking for precious free parking. We needed to be careful with money that day as we only had seven dollars in cash between us. The Dog, our most reliable source of pocket money, was pleading poverty.

Finding no street parking, we rolled north into Asbury Park, where, to our surprise, there was free parking right on the beach. No one we knew ever went to the Asbury Park beaches. As Kevin parked, I asked, "Hey, where are the mom and pop groceries? I only see dance clubs."

The mom and pop groceries were important because the mandatory beach-day snack was Yoo-hoo and Funyuns, which were only sold at the little stores. Kevin shrugged and concluded, "No groceries on the boardwalk just means no New Yorkers at Asbury Park beach. No downside to that, eh?"

I nodded and followed Kevin onto the beach. The Dog followed a little behind, and I heard him mutter, "Hmm, night clubs on the boardwalk—hmm, indeed."

A bit stir-crazy from the long quest for free parking, Kevin and I dropped our towels on a patch of unclaimed sand and dashed into the water. The surf was rough that day and we were soon bodysurfing with two guys in their twenties. I caught some waves just right and glided to the beach on top of them; I also caught some wrong and was pitchforked around—the same with Kevin and the older guys. There was plenty of banter and bravado as we tackled each other in the powerful surf and crashed together onto the sand.

I had finished a good ride and ducked under an incoming wave when I heard Kevin yelling at the two older guys. As I swam toward them, I saw Kevin with one of the guys in a headlock. He was repeatedly punching the top of the guy's head with his free hand. The other guy was trying to pull his friend free and calling for help. Every few seconds, a wave knocked each of them off balance and then rhythmically rebalanced them.

"What the fuck's going on?" I shouted as I came closer.

"This guy *touched* me." Kevin responded as he swung again.

I wedged myself between Kevin and the two guys, and took a couple of swings at them myself. I started shouting "Out, out, damn fag!" to the two guys (Kevin and I were reading *Macbeth* in English). This line, when repeated, made Kevin laugh and he let up. The less-pummeled guy threatened, "I'm getting the police." The two guys paddled toward shore.

We ran back to get our stuff. The Dog, still on the spot where we dropped our towels, smiled as we came sprinting toward him. In a wry tone he asked, "Are you ready to go yet?" We were in the car and driving fast within five minutes.

On the ride back, I unintentionally set Kevin off by suggesting that the gay guy's contact was solicited. Kevin and I still argue about what I said, but I think it was a pretty harmless quip along the lines of, "You know, Kevin, next time you should just place a personal ad in the *Village Voice*."

Whatever I said, it started Kevin shouting all kinds of really bad, homophobic things. He pulled off onto the shoulder, ran around the car, opened the door and pulled me out. He was within an inch of pummeling me when the Dog stuck his head out of the car and called out, "Hey Kevin, don't drop the soap in the shower tonight, at least not if your mom's boyfriend is around. He told me you have a tight ass and a real 'purdy' mouth."

Kevin shouted, "Shut up, Shylock!" and crammed a half-dozen anti-Semitic slurs into his next breath. But then Kevin started laughing. His relationship with the Dog was combustible and they went through short stretches of hating each other. But the Dog's lack of deference for Kevin's toughness earned him leeway no one else was granted. In this case, the Dog's big mouth saved my ass.

Versions of the story of our misadventure at the gay beach in Asbury Park have been told and retold so many times over the last twenty years that I no longer easily distinguish fact from fiction. In Kevin's version, he suggests that the Dog knew about the gay beach and steered us there, but I don't believe that. I do, however, think it's true that the Dog recognized that we were at a gay beach early on and let things play out for his own shits and giggles. Whatever the case, the version of the story as told above is stripped of the lurid, stupid, and homophobic hyperbole that was layered on with subsequent retellings. If this story plays into any unfortunate stereotypes, I regret it.

———

AFTER HIGH school, Kevin enlisted in the Air Force and became a nuclear missile technician. He spent five years watching dials and performing routine tests all day in a missile silo somewhere in the Dakotas. He ended up at a civilian nuclear power plant in Byron, Illinois with the same job—nuclear safety technician—as Homer Simpson.

Byron is a nice-enough small town on the Rock River in rural northern Illinois. Kevin alleges that Byron is home to a famous "Turkey Testicle Festival" where the residents eat the pickled testicles of turkeys from the town's biggest employer, a turkey poultry farm. When I visited Kevin in Byron, I found no evidence of turkey testicles being eaten, nor can I find anything about this odd tradition on the Internet. But Kevin says it's a big annual event and I am in no position to argue.

We see each other when he returns to New Jersey annually to visit his mom for Christmas. In between, we email each other strange and funny things. I consider him a close friend; he considers me the same, but reliably complains, "Duff, you have become such a pussy" when I don't indulge his latest adolescent idea.

Despite this, in the last five years, I have turned Kevin into a little bit of a reader—a big deal considering his long history of boasting proudly that he would go his entire adult life without reading a book. It started with me giving him a copy of James Gunn's *The Toy Collector*, a violent, brilliant raunch-fest about screwed-up children turning into screwed-up adults. I called in a lifetime of favors to get him to read it. Kevin will never admit it, but I know he liked it. Subsequent books given to Kevin have been Thom Jones' *The Pugilist at Rest: Stories*, Peter Carey's *The True History of the Kelley Gang*, Tristan Egolf's *Lord of the Barnyard*, and Sherman Alexie's *Indian Killer*. In the interest of appropriately targeting my audience, I make sure the selected books are violent and written in a testosterone-inflected voice. As part of the original quid pro quo, I agreed to go with him to an evening of hot-chick Jello-wrestling at a go-go bar in Keansburg. The annual tradition continues: he reads a book of my choice; I go with him annually to some woman-demeaning event at a bar of his choosing.

Kevin is still capable of adolescent rage and getting himself into real trouble. A few years back, he began one of his visits by grabbing my hand and pulling it onto his scalp. As my hand penetrated his graying mullet, he asked, "I have a hole in my head, wanna touch it?"

My fingers were soon enmeshed in a mass of soft flesh tissue. He explained: "A few nights ago, I was in a scrap at a redneck bar and was caught above the ear with a shot from a guy wearing a huge iron ring. The ER doc who stitched me up said the ring made a small hole in my skull that will never heal—too funny." Kevin then lowered his voice, "But don't worry, my half-spic amigo, I totally tuned up the redneck for popping a hole in my skull. He won't be hitting anyone else for a good long time."

More recently, for McGowan's fortieth birthday, Kevin and I took him to Atlantic City. We stayed at the Hard Rock Hotel and attended a Lou Reed concert (the guy most famous for singing, "Hey Babe, take a walk on the wild side"). Reed walked offstage three times during the show out of disappointment with the venue's sound system. This caused long delays each time as technicians fiddled with wires and called "check, check" into different microphones. McGowan, Kevin, and I—along with most of the audience—started booing Reed. When the show finally ended, there was little applause and no encore.

Five hours later, we were drunk and shooting craps in the hotel casino. I caught a glimpse of a familiar-looking older guy in a leather jacket and sunglasses. I called out, "Hey, it's Lou Reed!"

Kevin, drunk and irritated about being down $300, looked over at Reed and shouted, "I hate Lou Reed. Fuck you, Lou!"

He threw the dice from the craps table at Reed, hitting him in the chest. Within a minute, Kevin and I were ensnared in a net of uniformed and plainclothes security staff and muscled out of the casino. Because the bear-like McGowan restrained Kevin, Kevin didn't beat up any of the security staff. Thus, we were able to slink away without arrest.

Kevin has been married and divorced twice. I kid him about "going for the 'hat trick' on wives," and he tells me, "I'll never marry again." Neither of us believes that. He has a nine-year-old boy, Matt (named after me), from wife number one who he adores. He coaches Matt's youth hockey team and takes him dirt-bike riding on the weekends he has custody. Each year I buy Matt a nice Christmas present—most recently, a top-of-the-line graphite hockey stick.

Kevin regales me with stories of the annual pranks he plays upon Matt's mother each year near her birthday. My favorite was when Kevin hired a leg amputee to go into the shoe store she manages to buy shoes. As she rang up the amputee at the register, the man loudly demanded, "Where's the fifty percent discount on all footwear that I am entitled to under the Americans with Disabilities Act?" The amputee refused to leave the store without the discount.

Kevin's most recent prank was emailing the local congregation of Jehovah's Witnesses as wife number one, giving them her phone number and address, and requesting "their comfort and religious counsel."

We don't ever talk about wife number two. She was a nasty white-trash girl whom he married, by his own admission, "solely for her perfect ass," and over McGowan's and my vigorous protests. I don't know for sure, but I think he hit her. Kevin will not admit to it, but I know that wife number two exited his life suddenly and he was required to take a state-sponsored anger management class. A year later, Kevin remains under some kind of low-intensity state supervision.

DISCUSSION WITH LISA:

I sat down in my rocking chair. Lisa had the story out in front of her. She waited for me to speak.

"Can I infer from the silence you didn't like this one very much?"

"Well, if you're telling things straight, I think your friend Kevin probably has some painful, unresolved issues. I hope he's getting some help." Lisa looked down at a paragraph in the story that she had circled in red ink.

"Kevin's not so bad. Let me explain. Kevin's a great guy. He's a loving father and a loyal friend. He sends my son Jack expensive birthday presents every year even though he lives paycheck to paycheck. Jack thinks he's the world's coolest guy. Kevin performs more good deeds than anyone I know, and he does nothing to call them to anyone's attention. But he is, if you'll let me play shrink, id-driven. He acts impulsively without understanding the consequences of his actions. Any woman who is just getting to know Kevin loves him because he's outgoing, spontaneous, and funny. Cute too, I suppose. All women who've known Kevin for a long time, however, hate him because Kevin cannot control his fists, his feet, or his dick. His appendages control his brain, not the reverse. A lot of men are like this, including a recent, generally well-regarded U.S. president. Kevin is the blue-collar Bill Clinton."

I winked at Lisa, "By the way, he's single. Can I give him your phone number?"

Lisa laughed; it was the first and only time I ever saw her let loose. Her blazer pulled way back revealing a nice rack—it was a pretty sexy moment. (Hey, if I cannot drop a sexist, objectifying observation about Lisa into the chapter about Kevin, where can I?) But ten seconds later, Lisa was an asexual shrink again.

"Did you notice that I worked into this story something about the Dog saving my ass?" I asked. "I thought about what you said about how I was cherry-picking facts about the Dog. I figured I owed you something that showed the Dog in a moment when he was not a total dick."

"Yes, I did notice a different treatment of the Dog, though I hope you know that I do not want you to manipulate what you put into these stories."

I nodded. "I understand that. I know you're not going to force me anywhere I don't want to go. I guess I never would have said something like that three months ago." I grinned, happy with myself. "I am becoming your favorite nut, huh?"

"Among them," Lisa answered.

"Good, then this is the right time to discuss your discounted head-shrinking fees for preferred clients."

"I disagree. Instead, I suggest you focus on your next story." But Lisa's tone was lighter than her word choice.

"Okay, I'm ready to write about the Dog."

12

The Thinking Man's Bully, a.k.a., the Dog

When I was four years old, my parents took me down the street to stay with the Rosen family, and left me there for the entire day. I cried the whole time. The Rosens had a skinny boy with narrow eyes named Martin. My first memory of Martin is him taunting me, "Why are you crying? You're a crybaby. Wah-wah-wah." In the succeeding years, Martin Rosen and I were frequently deposited at each other's house and learned to get along.

By age eleven, we had been carpooled to a half-dozen activities together—basketball, soccer, ice skating, Little League, Cub Scouts, and guitar. Martin hated each, and was vigorous enough in his protests to avoid repeating any of them. I copied this behavior and my parents, dreading sole-driver responsibility, followed suit in letting me drop out of each activity.

By thirteen, Martin and I exhausted the circuit of common after-school activities. As other children continued getting shuttled around, he and I were latchkey kids with free afternoons. We entertained ourselves by finding spare coins in our houses—checking behind seat cushions or gently pinching our parents' change collections—and roller skating up to the 7-Eleven. There, we'd buy a candy bar and a comic book starring a conflicted brute like Bruce Banner (the Hulk) or Ben Grimm (the Thing). If we broke something that day, such as a glass bottle or the bike of a boy we didn't like, it was a particularly good day. Martin received a hockey stick as a birthday present when he turned twelve, and started taking it with him to enable acts of greater vandalism. He also started stickhandling a street hockey-ball. I told my parents I wanted a hockey stick and it promptly materialized. We started playing mini-hockey games against each other daily.

Martin hated the name Martin. He spoke his name only in Mel Blanc's monotone Martin-the-Martian voice.[1] He noted, "Only Martian Overlords—like my parents—are sinister enough to inflict the name Martin upon a defenseless child." One day, he renamed himself "Mad-Dog" after the AM sports radio personality, Chris "Mad Dog" Russo, whose apocalyptic rants about New York sports teams appealed to him. Always prone to overreact to petty offenses, Martin high-sticked and elbowed any boy in our hockey clique who called him Martin. "Mad-Dog" was shortened to "Dog" or "the Dog," and the name stuck. The Dog and I founded an after-school roller hockey cult and, by freshman year, ten or twelve boys gathered on most afternoons at Freedom Tree Park. We had great games.

That spring, the Dog nagged his parents into coughing up eighty-five dollars, and he entered a team into the Freedom Tree Park spring/summer Roller Hockey League. At the time, the team consisted of four players—McGowan, Kevin, the Dog, and me—and we recruited a half-dozen beginners at the last minute to round out the team. The Dog named our team Diamond Smiles in honor of the debutante in the Boomtown Rats song of the same name who commits suicide as a final slap at her superficial peers. Lacking a business sponsor or uniform, the Dog bought ten irregular Barry Manilow concert T-shirts for twenty dollars at the Englishtown Flea Market. We loved wearing these shirts and drawing looks from all the other teams with real hockey jerseys. Diamond Smiles went 1–11 that season, but earned a reputation for physically punishing opponents and stretching the rules. We

---

1. Mel Blanc did nearly all of the voices for the Warner Brothers cartoons, including Martin the Martian, an inspired foil to Bugs Bunny.

played for two more seasons. It was the only activity we ever repeated.

Based upon our common love of hockey, our early childhood companionship, and the sheer amount of time we spent together, everyone called the Dog my best friend, and vice versa. Neither of us disputed it, so it became fact. The Dog once said, "McDuff, we must act as best friends because the world is watching and we dare not disappoint Boutros Boutros-Ghali." The Dog was so amused by the name of the U.N.'s top guy that he introduced himself at parties by saying, "Hi, my name is Boutros Boutros, but you can call me Boutros. Or maybe I just stutter." He'd then reliably add, "And this mope over here is McDuff, my best friend by public acclamation."

While the Dog was funny and an always available playmate, I never felt close to him; maintaining a relationship with him was always complicated. The world thought we were best friends, but I had my doubts.

———

THE DOG boasted about being "unstuck in time, unburdened by convention, and liberated from fact." I always suspected that he stole this line from somewhere, but never proved my suspicion.[2] He always had a new story about one of his late night bus rides to the New York City Port Authority Bus Terminal. They often went something like this, "Duff, last night I made it to the Port Authority about midnight, and bought a gyro. I found Shaky, my Jamaican friend, and smoked a mega-doobie with him in the men's room. I then walked around the bus station, and talked to freaks for a few hours. I caught the five AM bus home just in time to shower, smile for mommy, and walk to school."

Over time, the Dog's stories centered on three characters: Shaky, the seizure-prone, Jamaican pot-dealer; Wesley, a bipolar poet angry at the world for denying his claim to the throne of the

---

2. Kurt Vonnegut's Billy Pilgrim character in *Slaughterhouse-Five* was "unstuck in time," but the rest of the line is not attributable to Vonnegut.

African Yoruba tribe; and Brownwyn, a wheelchair-bound older woman from a blue-blood family, who liked grabbing at the Dog's crotch. Though almost certainly lying about many of the details, the Dog demonstrated an ability to tell stories entirely consistent with previous ones. Desperate to catch him in a lie, I'd probe the Dog on a detail to one of his stories months later—"Hey Dog, I was thinking about that guy, Wesley, descendant of the last king of Nigeria. How's he doin'?" But the Dog always thwarted me with perfect recollections of his long-ago lie, "No, McDuff, Wesley's Yoruba. There was never a king of Nigeria; it was invented by the Brits. Wesley's fine. He frequently asks me about my half-Puerto Rican friend in Jersey with the low IQ." I never trapped the Dog.

The Dog never slept, or at least slept far less than any normal person. It seemed that no matter how late I passed his house, there was a light coming from the small basement window in back. Each time I looked in, he was playing Atari hockey against the game system or watching a sitcom rerun. I even set my alarm for two or four AM on different nights to see if the Dog was still awake—and most of the time he was.

When the Dog wasn't in his basement, I'd ask him the next day, "Did you finally crash and go to bed?" He always responded with incredulity, as if an admission of sleeping was a blow to his manhood. His canned answers were, "Not quite, McDoofus, I went to NYC last night." Or, "You show no faith in me, McDuff. I took the Route 9 Local to the White Castle in Old Bridge." If he ever slept in his bed, he never admitted it and I never proved it.

Sometimes when the Dog was in his basement late at night, I tapped on the window. He would look up, do a one-man version of the sports arena "wave" to greet me, and then let me in through the sliding door off the living room. There'd be a joint waiting just in case I showed up.

Late nights with the Dog included proctored "show and tell" sessions during which he lectured me about topics important to him. This included exposing me to R.E.M. when they were still a small-time alternative band, and introducing me to the challenging lyrics of Joe Jackson, Frank Zappa, and the Boomtown Rats. (Whatever else you want to say about Sir Bob Geldof, you have to respect a man who, at the peak of his career, sang self-deprecatingly about, "The big affair in the square when I was shooting my mouth off about saving some fish; why should that be construed as some radical's view or some liberal's wish?") The Dog also liked an eccentric a cappella band called the Bobs that performed manic covers of '60s songs like Cream's "White Room," and oddball originals like "Helmet," about an insane young man obsessed with protective hats, who finds peace by putting a colander on his head.

The Dog cherished his small collection of VHS cassettes. It included some terrific movies that flopped at the box office: Robert DeNiro's *King of Comedy* (about a terrible comedian who kidnaps the host of the *Tonight Show* to extort his way to comedic fame), Mickey Rourke's *Barfly* (about a violent alcoholic who just might be a brilliant poet), and Steve Martin's *The Lonely Guy* (a droll comedy about a lonely guy and his fern). The Dog loved certain old cornball TV shows and taped favorite episodes of *Green Acres*, *Sergeant Bilko,* and *Dobie Gillis*. He and McGowan memorized every line from *The Munsters* episode when Herman becomes a professional wrestler, but the Dog was indifferent to that show otherwise. And, of course, there were the old standbys: *Hockey Fights*, volumes I, II, III, IV, V, VII, and VIII. Volume II was our favorite because of the Dog's two favorite clips: Jimmy Mann's KO of Paul Baxter, and Willi Plett pummeling Ed Hospodor and then combing his hair in the penalty box. In a lifetime of searching, I still have never found a copy of volume VI.

Strangest of all were the Dog's late night lectures about the perfectibility of the brain. For years, he rode his bike to the Englishtown Flea Market on Sunday mornings and wandered the junk tables buying up anything under five dollars related to the human brain. Sci-fi books about Martians and evil scientists altering brains to make genius-servants were his most frequent purchases. But he also ended up buying a bunch of old anatomy books, brain models, and med school charts. This gave the Dog a strong grounding in brain science, circa 1955, which undergirded many of his lectures.

The Dog and I rarely discussed "serious" topics, and there were plenty we could have covered. Neither of us, for example, had the slightest idea how to begin—much less maintain—a romantic relationship. On the topic of girls, the Dog never showed any sustained interest. He stated as fact, "My Semitic 'good looks' make me ineligible for hot girls and I'm too young to chase fatties." But I think the Dog was just deathly afraid of girls. I remember that Kevin once pushed him to explain why he would not pursue Chrissy Conover, a nice girl who reportedly thought the Dog "was very funny and kind of cute." The Dog cut off the conversation by saying, "Can't be true. Cute girls only find guys like me attractive on the set of *Seinfeld*." The next day, the Dog egged Chrissy's house to assure his prognostication.

The Dog deflected conversations away from serious topics when I raised them. He'd say things like, "Don't kill my buzz with that Mike Brady shit." I once asked whether we were regarded as "losers" by our peers. He cut off the conversation by saying—and I think this is the exact quote—"You know, here I am busting my ass to shake you out of the suburbs, and you keep dragging me down with this 'it's so hard to be a teenager' bullshit. Who cares what the middle of the suburban bell curve thinks?" Most of the time, I was content to stick to the Dog's preferred topics: *his* eclectic music, *his* list of "movies that are too good to be commercially successful," and *his* hockey theories.

However, I did once get the Dog engaged on the subject of bullying. There was no grand plan to do so. We were talking about the lack of honor among certain NHL goons—players known for fighting and dirty play—who never dropped the gloves against the league's elite fighters, but actively provoked the finesse players into fights that could only have one outcome. The Dog cast fire and brimstone down upon the league's top villains—Paul Baxter of the Penguins and Ed Hospodor of the Flyers. I turned the conversation by asking, "Don't you think our bullying some of the boys at Freedom Tree Park is a little 'Baxteresque'?"

This set the Dog off. "Ya know, the older and stronger players—me, McGowan, Kopf, and even you, McDoofus—have a responsibility to toughen the younger and weaker ones. If a little rough stuff results in a few people who were never cut out for hockey finding their way to tennis, everyone is better off for it."

Then he stood up as he added, "If the term bully must be applied to me, at least call me 'a thinking man's bully.' Unlike you, I judiciously apply coercive resources to facilitate specific desired outcomes based on the accepted scientific principle of natural selection. You cannot comprehend the line between typical bullying and the activities in which I engage."

The Dog opened a drawer and pulled out an old browning chart of the human brain, with each lobe brightly colored to represent different kinds of brain function. "You, McDim, like most people, are dominated by the primitive parts of the brain here and here. But I have trained myself to be dominated by this piece of the brain, the Parietal Lobe—here. Humans are perfectible, the best of us could evolve into a super-species—the equal of the alien races in those old sci-fi movies."

The Dog then slipped into a 1950s-movie Martian voice, "The earthling McDuff is subject to the limitations of his primitive brain. But, I, the Thinking Man's Bully, have evolved to something far greater. Consider the Thinking Man's Bully's mercy [his exact word] towards the earthling, Bobby Flannery, in contrast to the purposeless bullying of earthling McDoofus upon earthling Flannery."

"Fine. But what about the other boys you've picked on? People didn't move their families to Morganville to have their sons bullied, did they?"

The Dog jumped on my retort as if waiting for it. He said, "Jesus Christ, McDuff, you and I are channeling the three centuries of blood in the soil of Morganville." He quickly ticked off a list of local atrocities: the burning of a Lenape Indian village by the Dutch in the 1600s, the arson of New Jersey's first Quaker settlement, land riots in the 1760s, Revolutionary War battles, retributive vigilante acts against Loyalists after the war, nativist attacks on Irish families in the 1830s, and a riot against German families in the 1840s." He then added, "And that just gets us to the Civil War. Shall I go on?"

I doubted that the Dog was telling the truth, and, if he was, wondered where he picked up this knowledge. The whole tirade was creepy. My neck hair stood up; the Dog's face was pink and his hands were shaking.

Whether the Dog actually believed the shit he was shoveling that night remains a mystery to me, though it was presented with enough passion to suggest he did. He apparently impressed himself with his phraseology during the rant. He consistently referred to himself in the third person as "the Thinking Man's Bully" in our late night conversations after that.

———————

THE LAST week of junior year was really bad for us. Hockey Rocky had kicked my ass in the Thrilla on Barzilla, and I simmered with anger at the Dog for wisecracking throughout. Then we were busted by Mr. Rosen for smoking a joint in the Dog's basement. Mr. Rosen, for whatever reason, was up at two-thirty in the morning. He must have heard talking in the basement, and came downstairs. My back was turned as I exhaled a toke out the little basement window, so I never saw him coming. Mr. Rosen didn't call the cops, but did call my parents—at two-thirty AM on a school night.

Given all the reckless, derelict shit in which the Dog and I engaged, it is amazing that this was the only time we were truly busted. For the Dog, the punishment was nothing more than a lecture. His parents smoked pot in their thirties and his older brother dropped out of college for a year to follow the Grateful Dead, so there was little room in the Rosen family for histrionics over a joint. But for my parents, especially Dad, pot smoking was the gateway to the world's three great evils: homosexuality, communism, and vegetarianism. He grounded me for the summer and took away the car keys—a death sentence for a Morganville boy.

The next day, in the cafeteria, I saw the Dog, Kevin, Fran from Brooklyn, and a few others talking in a circle. As I came closer, I heard the Dog joking about the pot-bust. "McDumb-ass will be riding his bike all summer long. There's justice to this. It was his fault we were caught. He was too stoned or stupid or both to hide the joint." The put-down bothered me, but the Dog's unilateral decision to make the event grist for the high school gossip mill made me wild.

Without making a conscious decision to do so, I pushed the Dog hard in the back of the head. He stumbled forward against a cafeteria table. He turned around with a stunned look on his face. After pausing for a second, the Dog gave me a weak two-handed shove that I deflected away. He shouted, "Lay on McDuff!"

I wheeled back and punched him. My blow landed on the upper part of his nose, powered by more than a decade of built-up resentment. I have never before or since hit anyone nearly as hard. He fell backwards against the table. I moved in to hit him again, but Fran from Brooklyn put herself between us, her slender body sheltering the collapsed Dog. She shouted to Kevin, who was watching the event motionless, "McDuff's gone crazy. Get him out of here." Kevin bear-hugged me and hustled me out of the cafeteria before I could hit the Dog again.

A DAY later, the night following the last day of school, the Dog blew his brains out.

He did it in the woods behind Freedom Tree Park at the entrance to Dukakis's Eyebrows. He was sitting in a lawn chair that he had stolen three months earlier from Barry Big-Hair's house. The body was discovered by a couple of jocks who alerted the cops. I never saw the body. When the news broke, nobody even knew the Dog was missing.

I learned of the suicide when a cop showed up at my door to ask me about the Dog. I was churning inside but remember forcing myself not to show any emotion. The cop even said, "You're taking this pretty well, son."

When my mother tried to comfort me, I pushed her arms away and shrugged, "Everyone knows the Dog does big, stupid things." I put on my skates and skated around Battleview Acres the entire day, not talking to anyone—not even McGowan or Kevin. This was partly because I was sad, but mostly because I had nothing appropriate to say. While the Dog was my best friend—at least by the way these things usually get measured—I was relieved by his death.

No one ever found out how the Dog got the gun. He usually had money in his pocket and contacts in the Port Authority bus station, so I assume it was not too hard for him. He chose not to explain himself through a typical goodbye-cruel-world suicide note, but he did leave a will (of sorts).

> Greetings People of Earth:
>
> The Thinking Man's Bully is disassociating from you puny earthlings. He urges no hysterics or disruption of suburban earthling norms; nor does he desire any of your barbaric end-of-life rituals. His Martian-Overlord parents are encouraged to let his best-friend-by-public-acclamation pick through said Bully's stuff and take any of it (despite said friend committing violence on said Bully). The rest can be disposed of as conveniently as possible. Hopefully, there's a do-gooder outfit that will take it away and find it useful.
>
> Unstuck in time, unburdened by convention, and liberated from fact,
>
> Martin

THE DOG was cremated. There was a short Jewish ceremony. I attended. The mouse on my jaw from the Thrilla on Barzilla had ripened to dark purple. I was quizzed about it at the funeral by Mr. Rosen, and I remember his suspicious look when I broke off the questioning by saying, "Look Mr. Rosen, there's no story here. I just got tagged during last week's hockey game."

Leaving the funeral service, I found myself filing out with a cousin of the Dog's who I barely knew. I spoke to her, "Hey, I jammed my finger playing basketball last night. Could you give it tug?" As she complied, I let out a large fart that echoed through the otherwise quiet hallway of the Temple Beth Shalom. Mr. and Mrs. Rosen scowled; so did my parents. I guess everyone did. When my family reached the car, Dad slapped me hard on the back of the head.

From that day through high school graduation a year later, people felt a need to express their condolences to me. Even now, twenty years later, when I bump into high school acquaintances, the condolences come out. I always respond politely.

I became a better and happier person after the Dog died. I went to college, straightened out as a student, and graduated cum laude. I earned a scholarship to attend grad school at Seton Hall University. There, I met a nice girl, Diane Ubanoski, and married her. We bought a house and had a child. I fell into a decent career path as a fundraiser/grant-writer for nonprofit organizations. (We use the term "development" within the fundraising profession to distract from the fact that we beg for money.) My efforts have kept numerous artistic and cultural programs afloat and kick-started some promising new ones. Diane and I patronize good causes and volunteer our weekend time generously.

My improvement as a person after high school graduation was part of a natural maturation process. There is a bell curve of stupid, cruel male behavior that ratchets up in the teenage years and ratchets down by the mid-twenties. But this only partially explains my evolution. To be blunt, the Dog was a terrible influence. He instigated much of the cruelty, sloth, and drug use that characterized my teenage years, and provided ideological cover for the rest.

The Dog's continued presence in my life would have worked against all that went right in my adult years. He would have hated Diane—her G-rated sensibilities, her pervasive niceness, her naïve materialism—and I doubt I would have told him to go fuck himself.

I am better off because of his death. Sorry if that's harsh.

DISCUSSION WITH LISA:

Lisa didn't even wait for me to sit down before asking the first question. "Do you think Martin Rosen was an unusually sad boy?"

"Well, he did commit suicide."

She waited.

"You're so serious."

She waited some more.

"Yes, he was very sad. The Dog had interests, but there's no evidence that he drew any real satisfaction from any of them. He was unusually timid in some ways. I suspect that he desperately wanted a few things—a girlfriend, for example—but he took actions calculated to prevent those things he wanted most. He was afraid to take a risk, afraid to be the butt of jokes. Think of the way he flipped out after losing the nose-size contest to Barry Rubin. His reactions were totally out of proportion. I think he wanted me as a real best friend, but he was such a dick. I could be his most frequent playmate, but never his best friend. He knew that. He also knew that on some level, I hated him. He was funny, but he was an asshole. There's always a place in male circles for the funny asshole, but no one wants that person as a best friend."

"Why was he like this?"

"It's hard to know for sure. When I think back on my childhood, I can recall the facts pretty well. But I was a troubled teen myself and observed the Dog through the eyes of a troubled teen. This limits what I understand about that time period. It makes *why* questions difficult. I know that the Dog was really, really smart—he had an incredibly quick mind. He could retain and manipulate facts like no one I've ever known. I know that fast minds are trouble when not focused on something worthy of their attention. In that way, I suspect the Dog's obsessions with hockey fights or *Green Acres* were the side effects of a super-charged brain searching for something to master, something worth mastering. Maybe boredom was at the root of his sadness."

"Okay," Lisa said, "but if boredom explains Martin's sadness, why do you think he was so scared to reach out and get the things that would make him happy?"

I rocked back in the chair. "The Dog knew he was smart. But he was insecure about many things—his skinny body, his Jewish roots, his fancy vocabulary, his ethical failings. He hated those rare occasions when people made fun of him. He hated, literally hated, being shot down by a girl or tweaked for failing at something. He hated getting punched in the face in front of Kevin and Francine because it showed him as a weakling. He was afraid of being seen as weak. He was afraid of so many things."

"Do you blame yourself for his death?"

"Ah, the long-awaited big question," I whistled. "I bet you've got some note-taking grad student watching through a one-way mirror."

"No, but there's a microphone hidden in my broach. It's recording you for my next lecture at the institute. Speak slowly; the audio isn't great on this thing." Lisa didn't smile, but I knew she was pleased with herself for the flash of cleverness, and for finally zinging me.

"You're starting to sound like me. I am so sorry for you."

I rocked in my chair a couple of times. "I no longer blame myself for the Dog's death. He was a dick—a bad person—not just to me, but to everyone. When I hit him, he deserved it. He killed himself—I did not kill him. I didn't even know he had a gun. But I am really sorry he died. He had so many talents, life could have turned out so much better for him. But I was a screwed-up teen myself. I couldn't get my own life straight, much less his."

I was amazed by how easily these words came out. For twenty years I told myself that the Dog's suicide wasn't my fault, but now I finally believed it. It really was not my fault.

"Wow! I can practically see the ghosts of Morganville High School leaving me; these things have swirled around in my head for twenty years. Hot damn!"

I paced around the office. "I never thought this head-shrinking would work—but I feel great. I need an 'I love my shrink!' bumper sticker."

I stretched out to give Lisa a high five, but she left me hanging. I bet there were times when Washington left Alexander Hamilton hanging too.

I walked to the window and looked out. "Let's start talking about Jack."

~ The Book of Jack ~

13

Jack & Jill Went Up the Hill
(and There They Met Boo Radley)

Jack's best friend as a young child was a girl his age named Jill Silva. The Silvas lived two houses down the street. There were only two other young children on the street. There was Janey Silva, Jill's toddler sister, and there was an autistic boy named Russell Ridley, three years older than Jack and Jill. Jack and Jill rarely played with Russell.

Russell was big for his age. He was easily 100 pounds at age eight, barrel-chested, and more than a head taller than the five-year-old Jack (who was also big for his age). Russell had a shock of frizzy black hair and oval eyes that made him look like a Japanese animé cartoon character—of the tubby, comic-relief genus.

Russell's autism led him to repeat questions. He often asked Jack, "Why do you have no brothers or sisters?" I don't think Jack was especially bothered by the question; he answered Russell by restating something I once told him, "Brothers or sisters are pains in the butt—you get more stuff without them."

Diane, on the other hand, gave labored explanations to Russell's only child question. "God has different paths for every family. There's no perfect family size," she'd say at the start of one of her dissertations on family size. Russell was puzzled by Diane's monologues, so he repeated the same question to her—again and again.

I sometimes teased Diane about revealing to Russell the "real reason" that Jack was an only child. A year after Jack was born, I went off and got a vasectomy without consulting her. Diane and I were going through a rough stretch and I was having doubts about our marriage. Another child was out of the question.

We had met ten years earlier. I was a starving twenty-four-year-old graduate teaching assistant for the mandatory Freshman Lit class at Seton Hall University. Diane was a freshman with strong basic writing skills, but no capacity for literary criticism. She was a tall nineteen-year-old with a curvy, if slightly heavy, figure. She cooked wonderfully (still does) and many of our "dates" consisted of her cooking for me in her dorm's congregate kitchen. Dinners with Diane highlighted my week. During the four years we dated, I spent almost nothing on her, but she never made me feel guilty. As long as I was faithful (always have been) and willing to commit to a long-term relationship, that was enough for her.

Diane liked my highbrow stories, or perhaps she just liked dating someone capable of highbrow stories. She certainly liked telling people her boyfriend was a grad student. The key people in my life split over Diane: McGowan liked her because she fed him mountains of delicious food; Kevin didn't because she discouraged me from misbehaving. My mother liked Diane because she was sweet; my father didn't because (in his words), "She's only in college to avoid working." At Diane's request, I put a ring on her finger when she graduated. After investing four years in me, she deserved it.

When Jack was born, or perhaps *because* Jack was born, we grew apart. I was reading Nobel laureates William Golding and J. M. Coetzee, while she was reading bodice-rippers and trite biographies about Oprah and Barbara Walters. With the exception of *The Godfather*, there were no movies we could watch together. I wanted her to go back to work—she taught kindergarten for two years before Jack was born—to bring a little more income into the household. She believed Jack needed a stay-at-home mom. I thought her argument was motivated by her fundamental laziness; she thought my argument was motivated by my arrogance. Neither of us was entirely wrong.

If I ever was in love with Diane, it ended when we started fighting about Jack, money, and my intense dislike of her favorite TV show, *Friends*. I could not bring another child into the faltering marriage. The night of the vasectomy, she cried and yelled as I ate painkillers and iced my raging testicles with a bag of frozen peas. From my half-stupor, I made light of the situation and talked up "the lifetime of hassle-free sex" it insured. I borrowed the line from the old Johnny Bench Krylon spray-paint commercial: "No runs, no drips, no errors."

Diane and I toughed-out that difficult period and stayed together, but by then Jack was becoming difficult and we were both well into our thirties. I shut down any conversation about vasectomy reversal by using the feminist line, "my body, my choice." Diane eventually dropped the subject.

Rose Silva (Jill's mom) was very, very *nice* to Russell Ridley. Rose once asked Russell, "Do you know what snow is made of?" When Russell responded quickly, "Frozen water. It is made of frozen water." Rose gushed, "You are such a smart, smart boy, Russell. Here's a cookie." The condescension turned my stomach, but Diane, who should have known better, pretended there was nothing wrong with Rose's stupidly simple question and the cookie reward for the slow boy. Diane sometimes read to Russell and taught him simple card games, but only on the afternoons I was off somewhere with Jack.

The Ridleys invited Jack over to play with Russell many times, but Diane always had an excuse, "Jack's getting over a cold" or "I need to take Jack shopping for new shoes." Jack attended Russell's annual birthday parties, but Diane always hustled him away the moment the crowd of children thinned. When Russell walked over while Jack and Jill were outside, Diane or Rose Silva closely monitored the situation. More than once, I spied out my window at Rose Silva, as she was spying out her window at the children.

In fairness to the moms, Russell was not always easy. In addition to endlessly repeating questions, Russell lapsed into calling Jack and Jill favorite television characters, usually romantically involved couples like Sam and Diane from *Cheers*, or Spider-Man and M. J. Watson from the Amazing Spider-Man cartoons. "Are you two going to get married?" "Do you love each other?"—he asked the children again and again. One afternoon Russell kept asking Jill, "Why do you have no penis?" but Jeanine Ridley (Russell's mom) intervened and that particular question was never repeated.

The oft-repeated questions did not bother the children—Jack loved being thought of as Spiderman—but the vaguely sexual content of these questions from the oversized retard played on sad stereotypes in the heads of Rose Silva and Diane. I told Diane, "It is ignorant and ugly to believe Jack or Jill are endangered—particularly in a sexual way—by eight-year-old Russell." Diane denied having any such fears.

I saw right through Diane's walling-off of her son from Russell. Diane countered that my sarcastic language about Russell (sometimes I referred to him as "Einstein" or "the Boy Wonder") was worse than her condescension. Of course, my statements were always said in jest: I always believed Russell an appropriate playmate for my son. However, my sarcastic names for Russell produced a bad result. One day, Jack overheard me refer to Russell Ridley as "Boo Radley" (the retarded character from the book, *To Kill a Mockingbird*). Jack had no idea who Boo Radley was, but liked the nickname and started calling Russell "Boo Radley," and Jill followed suit. I told them to stop, but to no avail. For years afterward, Russell was called "Boo" by all of the kids in the neighborhood. I was the cause.

———

JACK AND Jill played together on most days after kindergarten—sometimes at our house, sometimes at the Silvas, and sometimes outside within view of the moms. Jill was small and like many small children, she was particularly well-coordinated. By age five, she was riding a bike, catching a ball, and skipping rope. Jack kept up as best he could, but Jill's superior coordination (and bossy personality) made her the natural leader.

On many sunny afternoons, Jack and Jill—or more properly Jill and Jack—explored up and down our street. Jill took off on her bike and Jack trailed behind in his Big Wheel three-wheeler. At the south end of the street there was a cul-de-sac with a stream behind it. On Saturday mornings, while Diane was at yoga, I'd give Jack his little pail and tell the children to "Go on safari at the brook." Jack and Jill came back an hour later with a frog or a box turtle in the pail, and everyone considered it a great morning. The day the children brought back a small snake in their bucket, Diane freaked. Jack and Jill no longer went exploring in the brook. However, they still explored the rocky hill at the north end of our street because the hill was visible from the back window of our kitchen, and the wildlife-trapping opportunities on the dry hill were more limited.

On the days I was charged with watching Jack and Jill, I usually sent them up the hill, made myself a snack in the kitchen, and sat down at the kitchen table. There, I kept one eye on the kids through the back window and the other eye on the newspaper. One morning, Jack and Jill went up the hill and met Russell; the three of them played for an hour together. Rose Silva eventually saw the three playing together unsupervised and went running up the hill—she came back with Jill a few minutes later.

Diane came home a half-hour later and asked me about Jack. I was reading the conservative columnist, George Will, at the time, and thought it was more important to discuss Will than answer her question. As usual, Will was wrong that day, but brilliant in his wrongness. He had written a column about the sublime beauty of baseball and the brutishness of football. When Diane came in, I read her Will's line about the NFL: "The National Football League combines the worst two elements of contemporary American society: ritualized violence and incessant committee meetings."

Diane said "cute" and asked about Jack a second time. I motioned to the hill.

She looked out, saw Jack and Russell, and then excitedly asked, "Where's Jill?"

"Rose Silva pulled Jill off the hill a half-hour ago."

Diane amped up into that strained pitch only women can hit, and that they only hit when they are upset. "You mean *my baby's* up there with Russell alone?"

My response was probably unhelpful, "Yes, but don't worry. I told Jack that Russell was not allowed to penetrate his anus unless wearing a condom."

Diane glared at me and flew out of the house screaming Jack's name. I watched her sprint up the hill. When she reached Jack she hugged him hard enough to crush his spine. Apparently, Jeanine Ridley heard Diane shouting and ran up the hill too. Through the kitchen window, I observed the two women exchanging words with postures that suggested great mutual discomfort

---

A CLOSE reading of the Frankenstein story reveals that the real villain is not the monster, but the torch-wielding villagers who ignorantly forced the monster into isolation and self-loathing. Only then does the monster turn homicidal. The stain on me for not standing against the torch-wielding villagers of East Princeton, and allowing Russell to grow up walled-off from the neighborhood children, is among my most unambiguous sins. The fact that Diane and the Silvas never owned up to their wrongness casts shame on them, but grants me no absolution.

The Silvas relocated to Arizona years ago. Russell is now nineteen years old. He lives at home and participates in some kind of county-sponsored vocational program. I see him in green coveralls waiting at the corner on weekday mornings for the county van to pick him up. After years of mother-enforced separation, Jack has befriended Russell. When he sees Russell, he stops and talks with him. Once in a while, Jack gets a movie from the 7-Eleven, and goes over to the Ridleys to watch it with Russell. I am proud of him.

That is the full extent of our contact with the Ridley family; they don't speak to Diane or me.

Discussion with Lisa:

As I settled into the rocking chair in Lisa's office, she asked, "You look happy this week. What's going on?"

"I think I'm beginning to prove to you, eh—prove to me—that I'm not such a bad guy. I think last week's story about the Dog demonstrates that, and this week's story offers further evidence. What do you think?"

I hoped for a smile or nod of approval from Lisa, but all I saw was icy neutrality. "Well, what I think is that this story is not really about your son. It is about your wife. Do you think this story is about you convincing yourself, and maybe me, that Diane's a bad mother?"

With a little squeak in my voice, I said, "I am not lying. There are no lies in this story."

"I am not saying you lied. And, for the record, I like both *To Kill a Mockingbird* and *Frankenstein*. But remember, you pick what you write about. You have a lifetime of memories to mine and you picked a story that makes your wife look awful. A week ago, you told me you were ready to talk about Jack. Do you think this story is about Jack?"

"Okay, I understand your point. The next story I write about my son will be primarily about him. For now at least, I'll let up on Diane."

Lisa then started discussing different schools of thought about how bullying behaviors get passed down through the generations. Blah-blah-blah. She talked with me about how we scapegoat—inferring, I imagine, that I was setting up Diane as the cause of Jack's later problems. Blah-blah-blah. My mind had left the office. I was already writing my next story in my head—I was writing about Jack's first bullying incident and my role in it.

14

Eek! A Greek!

Jack was seven when a family with a six-year-old boy moved in next door. "This is exciting news," I declared. Jack lacked boy playmates; most of the families on the block were older with college-age children, and Jack was getting too rough for playdates with Jill.

Our new neighbors, the Zachariadis family—three older daughters and a young boy—were Greek-Americans from Staten Island. It was raining hard when they moved in, so Diane and I watched from our front window. We exchanged amused looks when the zebra-striped sofa was unloaded from the truck and giggled at the avocado-colored Formica kitchen table that came out next. There were no professional movers—just a clan of Greek men of different ages running in and out of the large Ryder truck liked crazed ants. One of the men loudly ribbed the new homeowners, asking, "Why have you moved from somewhere to nowhere?" The men emptied the truck in ninety minutes. That night almost twenty cars lined our street. Greek music and shouts of "Opa!" went on long into the night.

Initial contacts with the Zachariadis family were positive. Diane brought them a big plate of brownies and introduced Jack to their little boy, Dimitri. Two of the Zachariadis daughters came by the next day with a huge casserole of moussaka—which Diane and I loved, but Jack refused to eat because of the eggplant. However,

the ways of the New Jersey suburbs were foreign to the Zachariadis family. In a year, they made many faux pas that rubbed my
family raw. These included:

- Not buying a booster sticker from Jack to support the
  Little League. Sure it was a twenty-five dollar annual
  shakedown, but all the other families on the block
  reliably purchased the sticker.
- Giving out lousy Halloween candy. Other families in the
  neighborhood reliably handed out Kit Kats and Gummi
  Bears by the handful, while the stingy Zachariadises gave
  out only a single unbranded lollipop.
- Parking their car in front of my house when the curb in
  front of their own house was conspicuously open. I had
  no interest in looking out each morning at *their* rust-
  spotted Nissan Sentra—with its little Greek flag hanging
  from the rearview mirror.
- Making no effort to maintain their yard. It became a
  breeding ground for dandelions. Invading seeds from the
  Zachariadis yard parachuted into mine that spring. For
  the first time in years, I was fighting dandelions again.

This proved to be the clinching offense. I steadied myself
for what suburbanites dread more than anything—confronting a
neighbor.

I rang the Zachariadises' doorbell. This produced a long
Mediterranean-sounding ringtone. I mumbled, "You can take the
Greeks out of Staten Island, but you can't take Staten Island out
of the Greeks."

Grandma Zachariadis answered, "Chh-ello."

I spoke slowly and loudly so she would understand, "G-o-o-d
m-o-r-n-i-n-g. M-a-y I s-p-e-a-k w-i-t-h B-o-b-b-i-s?" She frowned,
left me standing at the door, and went to get Bobbis Zachariadis,
the father of the family.

Bobbis arrived at the door looking drugged. It was almost
noon on a Saturday, so I theorized that he was sleeping off a
rough night. (Later, I was reminded by Diane that Bobbis was a
NYC subway train driver who worked a night shift and endured

a ninety-minute commute.) Bobbis came to the door in paint-stained sweatpants and an undershirt with yellowed armpits. It dawned on me that this was not a man who cared much about weeds in his yard.

I offered a hearty, "How you doin'?"

Bobbis nodded and responded "hello" as politely as his bleary eyes would allow.

"Bobbis, I want to talk with you a little about some, uh, things I am doing to keep my lawn healthy. Maybe you'd be interested in, uh, doing some of the same things?"

He gave me a puzzled look.

I continued, "It's already a little late in the season, but I think your yard would really benefit from a fertilizer with a tough weed killer in it. The Home Depot sells the big bag of Weed 'n' Feed for about fifteen dollars. It could be spread in about twenty minutes. You can use my spreader if you'd like."

Bobbis smiled and didn't say anything.

"Dandelions are a big problem to keeping a good lawn. You know, Bobbis, it took me three years to get rid of them when I bought my house. I'd hate to start fighting them again. The only surefire way to get rid of them is to dig them out one by one, making sure you get the central root each time."

Now Bobbis Zachariadis understood. I wanted him—after working a double-shift and driving ninety minutes because his wife insisted that a house in New Jersey was the good life—to spend the day digging little yellow flowers out of his yard. Bobbis opened up his eyes and said to me, "Thank you for this advice. Is there anything else, my good neighbor?"

Understanding the discussion was over, I said, "Nope. Thanks, uh, for the chat."

Bobbis smirked, put up his hand in an exaggerated goodbye wave, and closed the door. I concluded Bobbis was not interested in maintaining the street's property values, much less assimilating his family into the neighborhood.

JACK AND little Dimitri Zachariadis struggled with each other also. Jack loved his slingshot and horsing around; Dimitri liked playing quietly inside. Jack wore only denim and T-shirts; Dimitri wore wide-striped corduroy pants and bright button-down shirts. Clearly, Dimitri was heavily influenced by his three teenage sisters. I joked with Diane that "Dimitri was the first six-year-old pulled off the set of *Queer Eye for the Straight Guy*." I wondered aloud, "How does thick-necked Bobbis Zachariadis feel about the way his son is developing? I would never let that happen to my son."

The first time Dimitri came to our house, Jack taught him the game where one player rests his hands atop his opponent's, and the player on bottom slaps at the opponent's hands on top. Jack slapped slow-reacting Dimitri until his hands went red, and Dimitri left crying. The next time he came over, Jack demonstrated the karate moves learned at after-school lessons; Dimitri was kicked in the belly and went home crying again. When Jack went over to play with Dimitri and Dimitri's older cousins, Jack came home crying after one of the bigger boys pushed him off the high side of the Zachariadis porch. I was furious at the Zachariadises for not intervening, but told Jack, "Stop your crying—you're not a baby anymore."

Diane scolded me, "You sound just like your father."

———

THE NEXT weekend, while Diane was shopping and I was trimming bushes in the front yard, I was roused by the sound of Dimitri crying. I turned and saw the two boys in the street with their bikes. Jack was standing with his BMX bicycle upright, straddling the bike's crossbar. Dimitri was sitting in the middle of the street with his cutey-pie Wal-Mart bike splayed in front of him. He was howling something in Greek—I saw large scrapes on both of his knees.

Dimitri's oldest sister ran out of the house to console him. She was about seventeen and in full bloom; even with a stereotypical Mediterranean uni-brow, she was a full-figured beauty. She asked

Dimitri questions in Greek and, between sobs, he gave her short answers. She scooped up her skinny little brother in her big arms and glared at Jack as she carried Dimitri into their house.

I deduced that the boys had crashed bikes. Judging by the result, Dimitri fell pretty hard. I shouted over to Jack, "If your friend gets hurt, check to see if he's okay, and then get an adult." Jack shrugged and resumed riding his bike, making circles in front of our house. I returned to trimming the bushes.

Ten minutes later, I heard Dimitri calling from behind, "Mister Duffy, Mister Duffy."

I turned around and saw Dimitri with two large Band-Aids on his knees and a homemade ice pack on his elbow. His sister and Bobbis stood watching us on the Zachariadis lawn thirty feet away.

"I need to tell you," Dimitri started, "that Jack, um, um, rode his bike into me and knocked me down. My father says you need to punish him." I felt terrible for little Dimitri, but my anger rose at Bobbis for sending over his six-year-old son to tell me to punish my son. Which family was the neighborhood pariah anyway?

I dropped down on one knee so I could look at Dimitri eye-to-eye. "Dimitri, are you feeling better now?" He sniffed and nodded.

I put my arm on his skinny shoulder, "Good. You know that kids fall off their bikes all the time, but the brave ones get right back up and become awesome bike-riders. I bet you are a really brave boy, Dimitri." He nodded again.

I gave Dimitri a friendly pat on the butt to send him home. He took a few steps and then his father shouted something in Greek. Dimitri turned back toward me.

I paused. With some reluctance, I called "Jack, come over here."

Jack coasted in parallel to the curb, jumped off onto the sidewalk, and walked over slowly. He stopped about ten feet away from Dimitri and me. I motioned for him to come closer. Jack took two baby-steps. He kept his glance low.

"Jack, Dimitri tells me that you rode your bike into him and caused him to crash. Did you do this on purpose?"

Jack shuffled his feet and mumbled something.

"Jack, you need to speak up."

He spoke a bit louder, "Dad, um, we crashed, um, bikes, but, but it was an accident." Dimitri's eyes widened in disbelief.

I glanced over at the Zachariadis lawn and saw Bobbis's eyes fixed on me. I asked Jack again, "Jack, tell me what happened and tell me the truth."

Jack looked at the ground and then repeated, "Dad, uh, the bike crash was, um, it was, um, an accident." He then looked up a little and said, "But I am sorry that Dimitri got hurt."

I stiffened my voice and said, "Jack, please say that directly to Dimitri, not to me."

Jack looked at Dimitri and quickly said, "Sorry you got hurt."

I glanced sideways to confirm that Bobbis was watching me, and then said in a voice loud enough for him to hear, "Jack, go into the house now!"

I turned to Dimitri, "Buddy, I think you should go home now. Jack and I need to continue our talk inside." Dimitri turned for home.

When I came into the house, Jack was sitting at the kitchen table fiddling with an inch-high soldier. I asked Jack, "Are you thirsty?"

He nodded yes. I made him a glass of chocolate milk. As he finished, he asked, "Dad, can I go downstairs to watch TV?" I nodded yes.

A few minutes later, I heard Jack laughing at a Tom and Jerry cartoon from the basement. "Fuck you, Zorba." I mumbled.

THE BIKE accident happened ten years ago. The Zachariadis family still lives next door. Both families dutifully wave to the other on chance sightings, but we've given up any pretense of being friends—at either the parent or child level. Jack's dislike for Dimitri has fermented into a silly anti-Greek shtick. He says, "The greatest Greek-American is the Snuffleupagus"—the slow-witted elephant-like Muppet from *Sesame Street*. He gasps, "Eek! A Greek!" when he sees anything about Greece on television. I let it go because it is only an extended joke and doesn't represent any real bigotry.

The two oldest Zachariadis daughters are now married and both live at home with their husbands. The family now has four cars, one of which reliably ends up parked in front of my house every day.

While writing this story, I talked about it over lunch with Jocelyn Tso, an accountant in my office and, more or less, a friend. Jocelyn is a self-described "ABC" (American-Born Chinese) who tells bittersweet stories about growing up in the only Asian family on an all-white street. My favorite story is of her first boyfriend running out of her house when he saw Jocelyn's mother gnawing on a plate of chicken feet. As I told Jocelyn about the Zachariadis family and their inability to assimilate, she started chuckling.

Between laughs she said, "Your complaints are probably no different from those of my neighbors where I grew up. Matt, understand that in the suburbs, there's only a white way and a wong way to do things. Your Greek neighbors may be white to me, but to you they're just another dark-skinned immigrant family eating chicken feet. Cut them some slack, I bet they're nice people."

At my request, Jocelyn and her husband (a nice Jewish guy named Adam) took my family to a basement restaurant in Philly's Chinatown where almost all the customers were Chinese. Among other things, we ate chicken feet that night. There's not much meat on them, but otherwise they taste pretty good. Jack couldn't be coaxed into trying one.

Discussion with Lisa:

After last week's correction from Lisa, I hesitated entering her office—my feet just stopped moving and left me stuck in the doorway. I wondered, "Why does this person have so much power over me? How did I let this happen?"

Lisa saw me. Her stone-face cracked just enough to reveal a little sympathy. "Come in. Relax, I won't bite. Tell me about your story."

I hated appearing so timid. I forced myself forward. "I think this story takes a tough look at an early bullying incident by my son, and my role in it. I think this is exactly what you asked for last week. Right?"

"Yes, this story responds to points I raised. Your story doesn't make you look like a great guy—but you selected a story and voice that makes that impossible. But I've probably talked too much. What did you learn about your parenting of Jack from writing this tale?"

I slinked into my rocking chair, "Mostly, I think this story reinforced something that I have known all along—there were moments in Jack's development when he tried out bullying behaviors. I let him get away with it. Heck, I even let my dislike for Bobbis Zachariadis reinforce Jack's bullying. I guess I'm a pretty bad guy in this story."

"I suspect you are being pretty hard on yourself and a more charitable depiction of the same events is probably possible. Did you learn anything else?"

"I learned that chicken's feet look gross but taste okay."

I looked to see if my humor had amused her, but it didn't. Disappointed, I pushed forward. "No seriously, I think I gained some insight into the subtle ways that white suburbanites make life difficult for outsiders. I think I could be more tolerant."

"Can you use your new awareness as a springboard for reconciling with your neighbors?"

I thought about Lisa's challenge, but couldn't give her what she wanted. "No. There's too much scar tissue on that relationship. But I will try to let more things go. Can you live with that?"

"I can live with pretty much anything you tell me as long as you are being honest with me and honest with yourself. If this is the best you can do, okay. I just hope you stay true to your words."

I nodded, and we talked some more. But I kept coming back to whether I could be true to my words. Could I let the little affronts go? I knew the odds were better than fifty-fifty that the Zachariadis family would do something to piss me off again within the week.

"Any thoughts about next week's story?" Lisa asked as we wrapped up.

"Yes, I just hope you don't like the Dallas Cowboys."

15

If the Glove Does Fit, You Must Acquit

With the exception of Sunday morning church services, there is no single activity in modern America that tortures as many people each weekend as Little League baseball. This is particularly true of the age eight Pony League season, the year that players transition from the batting tee to coach-pitch. The central problem of Pony League baseball is that most of the players are incapable of hitting a moving ball, and the game consists of a million throws per batter before the coach concedes and trots out the tee. It takes two hours to play the typical three-inning game.

At any given moment during one of these games, nearly all the participants are miserable. For the team at bat, all children besides the batter are passing time by putting pulled grass down each other's shirts, making little roads in the loose dirt with their baseball gloves, or whining to their parents in the bleachers about "needing to go pee." For the team in the field, the catcher—invariably incapable of catching a ball—swelters under a ton of equipment, while fielders stare off into space and pick their noses. No matter, the ball is rarely hit beyond the pitcher's mound. Coaches in the field chide their young players to pay attention, shouting "baseball ready." Coaches in the dugout call out "good cut" to all batters regardless of how lamely they wave at the ball.

A quick scan of the bleachers reveals similarly dismal results: there's the gaggle of mothers gossiping about the family of any mother not presently among the gaggle; there are solitary fathers catching up on email via Blackberries tucked between their thighs—mistaken in the belief that people aren't noticing; and, finally, there are the put-upon older siblings chasing down ungoverned toddlers. Two things are clear about this all-American spectacle: no one is having a good time, and no one will admit it.

No one except my dear Jack, the speaker of unspeakable truths. Half-way through his first game, Jack complained loudly, "Baseball is boring; there is nothing to do except sit in the dugout." This instigated similar whines from other teammates—and pretty soon most of the kids on the team were complaining. As Jack stepped to the plate, I overheard one in the gaggle of gossiping moms say, "That Jack Duffy is just a troublemaker." When Jack smacked the ball into the outfield, she paused and faced the field, clapped enthusiastically, and shouted "Great hit, Jack!" Then she turned back to the gaggle and continued, "I'm just glad I am not that boy's mother."

As the games wore on from April and May into June, the situation worsened. Jack, two years into karate lessons, practiced his punches and kicks on teammates. More than once, he hit a teammate a little too hard, leading to tears in the dugout. After a few incidents, Diane was told to sit in the dugout when Jack is on the bench to prevent further problems. When it became clear to Diane that Jack was the team terror and a common subject of mother-to-mother gossip, Diane stopped attending the weekend games. It was my responsibility to attend the games alone.

There was one father who shared my disaffection for Pony League baseball—Rey Pageira. He had a daughter on the team who, besides Jack, was the only child who could hit a pitch beyond the pitcher's mound. This made Rey unsympathetic to the children who couldn't hit. Rey and I wisecracked through games like the slacker comedians from *Mystery Science Theater 3000*. Rey's one-liners drew from the rich comic vein of 1990s pop culture. Two of the remarks I remember are offered below.

- When observing a scrawny boy stepping up to the plate, Rey cracked, "That boy looks like Niles Crane—he holds the bat as if it were a lemon zester from Hammacher Schlemmer."

♦ When an awkward-looking, large-headed boy stepped to the plate, Rey whispered, "Look, it's Janet Reno. I bet she'll murder the ball."[1]

Rey was an aficionado of the O. J. Simpson trials. After a six year hiatus following his murder trial acquittal, O. J. was back in the news again, convicted of the wrongful death of his wife in civil court. Rey loved all things O. J. Thus, the Asian umpire in the baggy black shirt was "Judge Ito" and the league's only woman coach, a curly-headed brunette, was "Marcia Clark." Rey often reminded me, "O. J. has a million dollar reward for anyone who finds Nicole's real murderer. I sure hope O. J. gets that bad man one day."

I repeated Rey's best lines on the rides home for my own entertainment. Jack had no basis for understanding the O. J. trials, but repeated the wisecracks because they made me laugh.

JACK'S COACH was Dan Schulteis, originally from north Texas. The Schulteises had three children, the oldest of which was Jack's teammate, Jason Schulteis—a quiet boy with bug eyes and a chronic runny nose. Despite all of the extra time Dan spent with him, Jason went the entire season without hitting a pitched ball.

My family got off on the wrong foot with the Schulteises on the first day of practice. Jason showed up wearing a Dallas Cowboys T-shirt. Although only eight, Jack was well-trained by me to hate the Dallas Cowboys. So Jack immediately started picking on Jason—calling him "Cowgirl," "Texas-tit," and other names he had heard me shout at the TV set a few months earlier when the Cowboys beat the Giants. Dan intervened in a mild way by telling

---

1. Niles Crane, played brilliantly by David Hyde Pierce, was the fussy, elitist younger brother of Frasier Crane, on the television show, *Frasier*. Janet Reno was Bill Clinton's uncomely Attorney General.

Jack that he [Coach Schulteis] was also a Cowboy fan "and not all Cowboy fans are as bad as you've been told."

Jack replied, "Well, my dad hates Dallas! He says that they're not America's team, they're South America's team—because they're all cokeheads."

After practice, Dan asked Diane to talk with Jack about the mini-tirade. Diane reported this to me on her arrival at home and demanded, "Matt, you must do something to put your sports likes and dislikes in the right perspective in Jack's head."

I took Jack for ice cream that night. "Jack, I know it is kind of funny, but it really is not fair to pick on other children for liking the Dallas Cowboys. Some people, like people from Texas, can't really help it. They're born Cowboy fans and don't understand what they're doing."

Jack understood. He said, "What you mean is that some Cowboy fans are like Boo Radley—retarded and not able to know left from right, right from wrong."

I smiled, "Bingo." We enjoyed the rest of our cones.

JACK, JASON, and a few other children on the team had identical baseball equipment. This was because nearly all East Princeton families shopped at the same Target on Route 130, and the choice of equipment consisted of just one youth baseball bat and two youth baseball gloves. This led to numerous instances of children picking up and walking off with gloves and bats that belonged to teammates. Some parents thought this was fine and bought their children replacements without complaint. I was not in this group. Gloves cost thirty dollars and Jack needed to be accountable for his possessions.

Following one of Jack's games in which his team—amazingly— tied (all games were declared ties to preserve the kids' self-esteem), Jack came out of the dugout without his glove. I threatened, "You'll be sitting in your room the rest of the day without TV or dessert unless you find it." Jack ran back into the dugout and emerged with a baseball glove two minutes later. I was happy there would be no punishment.

As we walked to the car, I made some sarcastic comment about the game being a tie again, and lied about the improvement I was seeing in Jack's team. Jack shrugged as if to say "baseball sucks anyway."

Getting into the car, I saw the Schulteises emerge from the dugout. Little Jason Schulteis was teary and whining about being unable to find his baseball glove. I looked at Jack in the rearview mirror. Jack held up *his* baseball glove, and put it on to show me that it fit his hand, well, just like a glove. I let Jack see my suspicious look in the rearview mirror. He smiled and said, in a pretty good Johnnie Cochran voice for an eight-year-old white kid, "The glove does fit, so you must acquit." I laughed a little, and then muttered, "No justice for the Goldman family or Cowboy fans living in New Jersey."

We drove away.

Discussion with Lisa:

The session began with Lisa asking, "What's your deal with the Dallas Cowboys?"

I shrugged, "Ask your boyfriend. He'll understand."

"Don is not a football fan."

I gasped, "I'm sorry. But you're educated, young, and attractive; throw him back and hook a better fish."

"You have a strange way of complimenting a person, Matthew. I assure you that Don is a very nice fish. A minute ago, I asked you to explain your rather strong sports-rooting interests. Let's get back to that."

"Okay, but you asked for it. Men, well, most men, have passionate sports likes and dislikes. Our greatest passion is our favorite team, but a close second is a passionate hatred of the rival of our favorite team. Growing up, I watched the Cowboys kill the Giants twice a year—and listened to stupid broadcasters anoint Dallas

'America's Team.' This engendered a lifelong hatred of the Dallas Cowboys in me and the hearts of millions of good people across the country, not just Giants fans. Eagles and Redskins fans, though gripped by all kinds of sad delusions, still know enough to hate the Cowboys with equal passion as Giants fans. In recent years, the Cowboys have been good, but mostly because they draft and trade for criminals and punks. America's Team: my ass. If I could crash their team jet without facing murder charges, I'd do it."

Lisa's mouth hung open. "So let me get this straight. You'd crash a plane full of people because, as a boy, the Cowboys beat up on your hapless Giants?"

Within the echo chamber of fellow Giants fans, I have said dozens of times that I would crash the Dallas Cowboys team plane. No one ever raised an eyebrow. But Lisa's push-back made me reconsider the statement. "Well, I guess not. There are a few Cowboys who are not criminals—Jason Witten seems like a good guy, and you have to admire the way Marion Barber runs the ball. But I am less passionate now than I was as a younger man. Remember the term 'fan' is abbreviated from 'fanatic.'"

"Thank you for this moderate explanation, Osama Bin Duffy." Lisa leaned back, amused, allowing her cleverness to settle across the room. "Okay. Let's get back to your story before this discussion makes me quit the psychiatric profession. What about Jack? What does this story say about him?"

"It tells you, tells me I guess, that Jack was well on his way to being a bully and a problem by age eight."

"Is that the point of the story?"

"I suppose so."

"Okay. Does this tell us more than your story about the poor little Greek boy from last week? Can your next story take us somewhere new?" Lisa challenged.

The session continued, but my mind was racing, searching for a different topic for the next story. I settled on a story that would display a different side of Jack, and put Diane and me in a different light.

16

Mathematics and Math-Maddox

Jack failed seventh grade math. He was already in the lowest math aptitude group in school, so it was disgraceful for a smart boy like him to fail a course that could reasonably be titled, Math for the Nearly Retarded. I can only assume that he went the entire year without completing a single homework assignment or studying for a single exam. A couple of times during the year, the school sent home notices telling Diane and me that Jack was in trouble. When asked, Jack shrugged and gave one-word answers. The one time I pressed him, I was told, "Dad, I just aced the last quiz and should get a B for the quarter." I bought the lie. The B never came, the F did.

When I received Jack's end-of-year report card and saw the failing grade, I was not surprised. But I turned on the incredulity when I asked, "What the hell is this?"

He showed little emotion, "It's an F, Dad. It just happened."

When I showed Jack the accompanying letter stating that he needed to pass remedial math in summer school or repeat seventh grade, Jack cracked like an egg. "It's not fair. It's not friggin' fair," he sobbed and started crying, "that fat cow, Ms. Covine, hates me and never once cut me a break."

Diane cried with him, and was full of remorse about our alleged terrible parenting. According to her, Jack's trip to summer school was "a stain on the whole family," not just Jack.

I wasn't buying it, and yelled at Jack, "You are solely responsible for the situation."

————

Due to budget cuts, there was only one middle school in all of Mercer County offering remedial seventh grade math. It was Malcolm X Middle School in Trenton. Diane almost died when she learned that Jack had to attend summer school in downtown Trenton. Despite being the state capital and living only twenty minutes away, Trenton was another world to us—a strange dark place where poor black men drank malt liquor from bottles wrapped in paper bags. I never witnessed this occurrence, but the B-roll footage was shown again and again on the local TV news, so it became fact.

There were no options besides Malcolm X or repeating the grade. Diane and I braced for histrionics when we told Jack about it. To our surprise, the thought of attending an all-black inner city school did not faze him. Jack moaned about the loss of lazy days at the swim club, the long bus ride, and the lack of air conditioning, but that was it. Since I wasn't sure if he understood that he was going into the "hood," I blurted out, "Malcolm X is a black school where the kids get their lunches paid by the state."

Jack shrugged, "Good, they'll think I'm rich—in addition to being supremely cool."

Talking with Diane before bed that night, I told her, "I'm proud that our boy is not tarred by our generation's hang-ups about race."

The first week of summer school came and went without any big news. As usual, Jack was non-communicative, giving us no indication about what he was learning. However, Jack described his new classmates with the precision of an explorer returning to Europe with exotic tales of savage lands. "My class has thirty-three kids, twenty-three of them boys, all the kids except five are African-American. I am guessing that only one or two in the entire class are from two-car-garage families."

Jack described Malcolm X Middle School. "It's an enormous old building with real marble columns at the entrance and big, old red bricks. And get this, Dad, metal detectors were just put in after a gun was brought into school."

Jack liked the ritual of going through the metal detectors each morning. "It's cool walking up those steps each morning with really bad kids. The school's stone ground floor keeps the entrance cool even on the hottest days, but my class on the second floor is a sweat chamber."

According to Jack's reports, the only relief from the heat was a single oscillating fan in the back corner of the room. Jack told us, "The seat next to the fan is reserved for the 'alpha-boy'—me." By the end of the second week of summer school, Jack reported receiving nasty looks and verbal challenges from a big African-American boy who attended the Malcolm X school year-round. The large boy, named Jermaine Maddox, told Jack "to stop acting so big in my house."

Diane urged Jack, "Just give up the seat."

Jack repeated the advice given him by Uncle Kevin, "You can either get pissed off or pissed on."

I chimed in, "Uncle Kevin's right. You cannot give an inch to a bully."

Jack, already wise to the ways of boys, matter-of-factly talked about the "ritual" in which he and Jermaine were engaged, telling Diane, "Jermaine and I will have it out in the next week or two; sooner, if Jermaine puts himself in my seat next to the fan." Jack discussed his coming fight with Jermaine without malice. He slipped into the patrician voice of David Attenborough, the famed British naturalist and voiceover guy: "The coming clash between the two powerful young grizzlies is another of nature's duels between males seeking to establish primacy."

Diane frowned whenever Jack spoke like this, and made him promise not to "start anything." Jack nodded and said, "I'll wait for Jermaine to challenge me, but I will defend myself when the time comes."

I explained to Diane—yet again—the importance in male culture "of answering a challenge when called out."

She grumbled, "Men are such savages."

Jack and Jermaine fought the following week. Jack came home that day with the collar of his shirt torn, but otherwise looking fine. Jack never gave details when he beat up other boys. I doubt he inflicted any more damage on Jermaine than he had to—just enough to win. When I asked Jack about the fight, he smiled. With some prodding, the story came out:

"During class today, we were doing multiplication quick-answer drills. Even in my lame class, most of the boys have their multiplication tables memorized. But Jermaine Maddox and two other dummies don't know their times tables. They were forced to the front of the room where the teacher coached them through the rough spots. The rest of us watched and made faces at them. While this was going on, I cracked about this being a class for 'mathematics' and not 'Math-Maddox.' Other kids liked the joke and started calling out 'Math-Maddox' as well. He challenged me when class let out."

IN EAST Princeton or Morganville, Jack's victory over Jermaine Maddox would have ended the matter. Jermaine would have dutifully fallen in line. But things don't necessarily work that way among inner city boys. The next week, Jermaine jumped Jack from behind as Jack passed through the metal detector. Jack broke free and bested Jermaine again before guards separated them. Both boys were bloodied, and Jermaine was suspended for a week for instigating the fight. On his return, Jermaine attacked Jack again, this time with assistance from a friend who tackled Jack, allowing Jermaine to land several shots on Jack as the other boy pinned him against a bank of lockers. Other boys watched in a circle, not offering any assistance. After one last kick, Jermaine shouted at Jack, "This is my house. Don't come in here all proud of yourself—shit-for-brains."

Diane and I drove into Trenton that afternoon to pick up Jack from the hospital emergency room. Fortunately, the hospital visit was just a precautionary measure taken by the school. There was nothing in Jack's body broken in any substantial way.

Sitting in the emergency room in Trenton's Center City Hospital, I was aware that Diane and I were the only white people in the room. No one treated us badly, but the feeling of "differentness" was palpable. I was keenly aware of the Afrocentric magazines, the urban music playing quietly in the waiting room, and the Ebonic and Caribbean accents all around me. I started thinking about Stephen Fish. I wondered about the differentness felt by the son of an African-American scientist growing up in the white suburbs. Would he feel any more comfortable in this setting than me?

The assistant principal from Malcolm X met us. She expressed her "sincere regrets" for the incident and added that, "Jermaine and his accomplice will not return to Malcolm X." The assistant principal then told us confidentially that "Jermaine has been referred to the state's juvenile services division," although I don't exactly know what that means.

As for Jack, the several abrasions and bruises on his body healed before summer school ended, and nothing worse came from the fight. Jack passed remedial seventh grade math, and he was not held back.

Jack and Jermaine Maddox never met again. Though Diane shudders when I say this, I think the fights with Jermaine were a good experience for him. He surmised on his own that "Math-Maddox would have kept coming back, with a knife or a gun if necessary, until his dominance was established." This also taught Jack a little humility about the limits of his toughness, and also that East Princeton wasn't such a bad place.

I despised Morganville growing up—largely because I had no sense of the downsides of living in a more dangerous locale. The summer school experience in Trenton didn't turn Jack around as a student, but it taught him that white middle class suburbs like East Princeton are safe. In a Maslow's Hierarchy of Needs kind of way, safety is a big deal—something Jack now understood.

For all of his subsequent teenage sullenness and problems, Jack has never once complained about being raised in East Princeton.

DISCUSSION WITH LISA:

I wanted this session to be different from the last, so I started with a question for Lisa. "Do you think I'm gaining anything from these stories?"

Lisa looked at me. "I think I am supposed to ask you this kind of question."

"Probably true, but let me put you on the couch a little this week. Do you think I am gaining anything from these stories?"

"Okay, I think you are writing these stories to inform yourself about your son's troubles by building out key moments in his childhood. They illustrate that both you and Diane made mistakes as parents. I hope you know that all parents make mistakes. But this week's story is not about any big parenting mistakes. What do you think it is about?"

I thought about her question, and opened my mouth to respond. Then I stopped, "Damn, you're good. I am back on the couch, and you're in control again." I laughed, "Fine, I will reassume my secondary role. Dr. Melfi was always ten times smarter than Tony Soprano."

Lisa was unresponsive, as usual. After a short silence, she said, "Okay, tell me what this story is about."

"I think this story is about my son's bravery and, if you'll indulge the term, nobility. Jack went into a potentially hostile environment without any racial baggage. He behaved with honor against a dishonorable foe—and he came away with some appreciation for the safe life that Diane and I have created for him. Jack's a good boy in this story."

"Can you figure out why I might disagree with that characterization in this story?"

"Well, um, I don't know. Can't you just tell me?"

The boulders came tumbling off Mt. Rushmore. "By your own narrative, Jack provoked a fight with another boy on that boy's 'home turf' and he never once—as best I can tell—did anything to ratchet-down the bad situation that he saw coming. He never involved teachers or others who could have helped. Events spun beyond the control of his Rambo pose, and he nearly got himself seriously injured. This does not cast his foe, Jermaine Maddox, in a good light. But I would like you to think about whether your son's martial sense of honor—which you apparently support—is helpful to either of you."

Despite being lambasted by Lisa, I smirked. Lynette could have said the same thing to me; Diane would've tried to say the same thing, but the words would have come out wrong. I realized that this week's story had stumbled into the *Men Are from Mars, Women Are from Venus* conundrum. Any man, well, any real man, would conclude that Jack's conduct was admirable, but most women wouldn't. "So, you didn't much like this story?" I asked.

"Do you think this kind of simplistic question is helpful?" Her tone was more sympathetic than her word choice.

I thought about her question, then challenged her, "Actually, it could be argued that this is one of my more revealing stories. It sheds some light on my need to have a tough son—and my continued need to celebrate his toughness. This ties into Jack's, and I guess my, continued admiration for Kevin."

I saw her nod slightly.

I thought about that understated nod of approval through the week as I wrote a story that fully explored the "toughness" issue.

17

The Karate Kid

I started Jack in karate when he was six years old so he could defend himself against older bullies. Diane was skeptical; she wanted Jack in piano lessons. Since he was already playing soccer it was either karate or piano, not both. For a few days, we smoldered at each other by day and rehashed the piano vs. karate debate by night. I argued, "Karate isn't really about fighting, it's about self-discipline and focus. Jack is spacing-out in school—the discipline of the martial arts might help." Diane gave in.

I left work early to take Jack to his first karate lesson. I drove him to Tiger's Gym, at a strip mall a few miles from our home. I saw posters of tough-looking Asians as I entered the storefront, and children of different ages play-fighting and simply playing on the thick gym mat. There were banal power words in big capital letters on each of the four walls: RESPECT, FOCUS, DISCIPLINE, and STRENGTH.

A white guy in his twenties came over to us with a small robe and introduced himself as "Mr. Jim." We shook hands, and then he dropped to one knee and started talking with Jack about a martial arts-based cartoon, Avatar, that Jack apparently loved. I liked Mr. Jim immediately because he was clearly good with children; I was also glad that there'd be a young white guy helping out with the karate lessons.

I was disappointed when the lesson started ten minutes later. Mr. Jim was the only instructor. Where was the wisdom-spewing old Chinese master?[1] My disappointment grew as I watched the lesson begin with calisthenics and somersaults straight out of public school gym class. Over the next hour, Mr. Jim taught karate basics—thrusts, blocks, turns, front-kicks—and performed various stunts and pratfalls in between drills to keep the kids happy. The young warriors spent the last ten minutes of their "karate lesson" playing dodgeball. I came away unimpressed. However, Jack was happy with it. So I kept quiet, knowing one disparaging word from me might lead to a piano-for-karate swap.

Six years later, Jack was the youngest brown-belt at Tiger's Gym. I was proud to tell this to friends and family, and dragged visitors to Jack's karate lessons so they could see the twelve-year-old brown-belt hold his own in sparring drills with boys four years older. To her credit, Diane also overcame her initial dislike for the martial arts, won over largely by what she called "Mr Jim's non-militaristic approach to karate."

As a stay-at-home mom, Diane shuttled Jack to after-school activities, including karate. So I never learned about the tournaments available to Mr. Jim's better students. But one week while Diane was visiting her sister in Maryland, I took Jack to karate. Mr. Jim passed around a blue sheet of paper on a clipboard at the start of the lesson advertising a full contact tournament in Albany, New York. He was chartering a bus for interested brown-belts. I signed up Jack immediately.

I excitedly told Diane the news on the phone that night. She was silent. Sensing Diane was angry at me for unilaterally killing one of our weekends, I explained, "I checked the family calendar"—a big desk blotter in the kitchen meticulously maintained by Diane—"and the weekend is wide open." But that didn't change the chilly silence coming through the phone.

---

1. Karate is actually a Japanese martial arts discipline.

Finally, she spoke. "I don't want Jack in a full contact tournament. He could get paired up against some big ape. He's only twelve. He might get hurt."

I explained all the reasons why this would be a great experience for him: "Look Diane, the bus ride with his mates will be fun for Jack. It will be a chance for him to meet kids from all over the northeast. And a win or two at the tournament will be great for his self-esteem." Diane was a devotee of the idea that high self-esteem is an entitlement of all suburban children, no matter how mediocre or boneheaded. I avoided discussing that it was a full contact tournament, and lied, "I talked with Mr. Jim about safety and protective gear at the tournament. I was told no one ever gets hurt."

Diane was not convinced, "These tournaments come around a few times a year and will again."

On this statement, I went ballistic, "Why'd you never tell me about these tournaments? Why do you make these decisions about Jack on your own? This is just another example of you making every decision about our son without consulting me. It is sinking this marriage." Inadvertently, I played the trump card in the argument.

A month later, at six AM on a Saturday morning, Jack, Diane, and I boarded a bus for Albany with Mr. Jim, twenty parents, and twelve karate prodigies. The parents settled in the front seats; the boys boarded next and moved toward the back of the bus. Jack came on last. He looked at the older boys in the back of the bus, and then asked Diane, "Hey, Mom, do you mind if I sit with Dad?" Diane and I looked at each other; she stood up and settled in a few rows back with another mother. Jack hopped over me and took the window seat.

I sat with Jack as we rolled up the New York Thruway along the Hudson River. As we passed signs for towns, museums, and points of interest, I took the opportunity to reel off what I knew about the Empire State and its great river. We talked about Robert Fulton's steamboat, the Erie Canal, and the Battle of Saratoga. I told him about the Dutch patroons of the 1600s who owned estates along the Hudson the size of small states, and the Gilded Age industrialists who built the nation's most ostentatious mansions on the river 200 years later. I told him about the great creative minds of the region before the Civil War: our nation's first great writer, Washington Irving, and our nation's first great art movement, the Hudson River School painters. We talked about the region's three presidents: the Roosevelts and Martin Van Buren, the eighth U.S. president.

Jack was still untrained in the teenage art of indifference, and I surprised myself with how much of my liberal arts college education remained within me. For me at least, it was one of the nicest blocks of time I ever spent with my son.

We rolled onto the State University at Albany campus, the tournament site. I told Jack, "All post-World War II state college campuses look the same: loop road, sagging campus maintenance, concrete academic buildings that could have been built in the Soviet Union." I wished aloud, "I hope you step it up as a student soon so you can win some financial aid and get into a private college where the environment is superior —to say nothing about the better alumni networking after graduation. If you worked as hard in karate as you did in school, you'd still be a yellow-belt." Jack didn't respond, but I could see that my words stung him. He turned, and stared absently out the bus window. My relationship with Jack changed in that moment: I took my first look at my teenage son—withdrawn and distrustful.

——◆——

ABOUT NOON, we parked outside an athletic building. Jack fell in line with the other brown-belts at the registration table. He was small in comparison to most of them (but at five-foot-five he was big for his age). I whispered to Diane, "These kids are all two or three years older than Jack."

Diane picked up on this too and made numerous comments to me like: "that brute better not hurt my baby" and "I am stopping the match the first time someone touches him." I felt a little queasy.

The matches started at three in a wrestling gymnasium with a few rows of close-in bleachers. The first few bouts came and went without any great action. A few of the competitors were very good, and knew kick-punch combinations beyond anything Jack could do; but other competitors seemed at Jack's level.

Jack's first bout was against a tall boy. As it started, Diane buried her head in my shirt and mumbled, "I can't watch." Five seconds into the match, the boy hit Jack, and Jack's poorly secured headgear pushed across his face. The ref stopped the match and readjusted the gear. Diane, still not watching, asked "What happened?"

I reported, "The boy nailed Jack in the head; they are readjusting his headgear."

Diane mumbled into my shirt, "You're a monster for doing this to my baby."

Jack looked over at me, stunned at being hit so hard so quickly. I shouted, "It's all right, Jack. Now you hit him."

As the match resumed, Jack planted a straight kick into the boy's midsection that knocked the boy backwards, and also knocked Jack over. The boy tried to hit Jack with a spinning kick, but Jack landed a short jab first.

And so it went for the rest of the bout. Jack took two more hard shots, but held the upper hand besides. Diane was even able to watch the second (and final) round of the contest and squealed joyfully every time Jack landed a blow. When Jack was announced the winner, we both cheered loudly.

Jack's second round opponent was also tall and had long blonde hair that hung well below the shoulders. Before the match began, everyone in the little wrestling arena could hear the opposing coach shouting with revivalist-pulpit intensity, "Take him down, take him down hard!"

Mr. Jim gave Jack his canned pre-match reminders. "Protect yourself, look for your spots, and have fun out there."

As the two competitors came onto the mat and bowed, Diane asked, "Is Jack fighting a girl?" Indeed he was.

"Poor thing, I hope Jack knows to take it easy on her." Diane gave me a look that suggested I was displaying my "Bobby Riggs tendencies" again.

As the match began, Jack swung lightly. The answer came back quickly. The girl hit him with two strong punches that backed him up; then she landed a perfectly executed spinning kick into Jack's chest that sent him staggering. Jack straightened himself and fired back at her, and the two traded blows briefly before she nailed him with another spinning kick that sent him backward again as the first round ended.

As Jack readied for round two, Diane and I shouted encouraging words. Diane reminded me, "Matt, this girl has both age and size over Jack. It's okay if he loses." I looked away and said, "I know that."

The girl came out quickly at the start of the second round. They started trading blows, with the girl getting the better of the action. Then she caught Jack with a perfect straight kick on the jaw, and he went down. My heart stopped. It was the only time I saw anyone hurt my son. And it had to be a girl.

Jack stood up and finished the round by protecting himself. As they took off their headgear, the referee raised the girl's hand. She wiped her sweat off with a pink towel and gave a playful, distinctively girly little wave to someone she recognized in the audience. Then she gave Jack a quick hug, and jumped in the air in celebration. Jack sulked over to Mr. Jim, who placed his arm on Jack's shoulder and led him over to us. Diane raced forward and hugged him so hard that I heard Jack's exhalation.

On Sunday, we watched the rest of the tournament. The championship matches were over by noon. Carrying our overnight bags to the bus, Jack and I walked past another group loading onto a bus bound for White Plains. A striking young blonde woman in tight jeans was on line waiting to board. She nodded toward Jack and called, "Good match yesterday. Stick with it, kid." The girl who beat up my son was a knockout—not even a little butch.

We were home by four. I dropped Diane off at home, and then took Jack to his favorite sandwich shop, Cluck U, near Rutgers in New Brunswick. We talked about many things over chicken sandwiches, but never mentioned the tournament.

A week later, Jack had an incident in karate with a boy named Jeff Zobel. The boy caught Jack with a good kick, and Jack went wild. Jack did not stop hitting Zobel even after the boy doubled over and Mr. Jim called the match over. Mr. Jim pulled Jack off the boy. After that, Jack was banned from sparring.

Jack quickly lost interest in karate and became friends with Joey Giovanni, the neighborhood troublemaker. I learned from Diane that Joey had been expelled from Holy Name, the local Catholic school, for mouthing off to a nun. He told Sister Mary Agnes, "Well, if God is everywhere, then he must be up my ass— and up yours." When he saw the nun sobbing later that day, Joey reportedly proclaimed himself "the Habit Breaker" in front of a cluster of consoling faculty. For this transgression and, no doubt, dozens of others, he earned a ticket back to the public schools.

The first time I saw the boys talking together, I overheard Joey razzing Jack. "Don't worry, Jack, you can kick the ass of any hot girl I know." Until then, I assumed that the match in Albany would stay a family secret.

———

FOUR YEARS later, Jack and I still had never discussed the tournament or the bout against the girl. That changed when I started writing this story. I took Jack fishing because I wanted to talk about the tournament experience with him when he was relaxed, happy with me, and lacking an escape route.

Jack was in a good mood when I raised the topic. I told him, "Your mother and I practically came to blows over that tournament." I gave him a smile.

"Well, that tournament was another great self-esteem boost for the son of the father of the year." Jack wasn't smiling.

DISCUSSION WITH LISA:

I started by asking Lisa about the expected snowstorm and the psychology of panic-buying. After a few minutes, Lisa said, "It is time we turned to your story, Matthew. We've discussed the coming 'storm of the century' long enough. Tell me about The Karate Kid."

"It's a very poignant tale. I laughed, I cried. Mr. Miyagi's bonsai tree was just so beautiful." I sassed about the recently remade cheesy movie of the same name.

I looked to see if my wisecrack got to her. No luck. She said, "No really, tell me about your story."

"Well, I thought a lot about our discussion from last week— about my need to have a tough son. Jack's experience at the karate tournament with that girl in Albany was the perfect vehicle for exploring this."

"And what did you learn?"

I thought about wisecracking, but I was already at my quota of diversions for the session. "I learned that I pushed my son to become a young gladiator, and that I was not helpful to him after he was defeated by a more experienced opponent who—regardless of gender—logically should have kicked his ass."

"Could you tell this to Jack now?"

"I don't think it would do any good. That was four years ago."

"Can you talk to Jack about the tournament now? He's a troubled boy who might want to hear that his father is okay with him getting bested by a female."

"Do I really have to?" I asked.

She remained silent.

I caved, "Okay, I need to talk with Jack about this."

The conversation continued, but I was already thinking about the next story, thinking about the events that led up to Jack's attempted suicide. It was time.

That week, I experienced writer's block. I started writing about the lead-up to Jack's attempted suicide twice, but deleted the file both times because it wasn't coming out right. I decided that there was a good transitional story needed first. I wrote it in one sitting.

18

The Wheels on the Bus Go
'Round and 'Round

The middle school bus hosts much of our childrens' worst behavior. I think this is attributable to three facts: The bus places stronger and weaker children in close proximity; the rides are repetitive, long, and dull; the bus driver is generally disinterested in the behavior of the riders. The following story about Jack at age fourteen is illustrative.

As the largest (five-foot ten and 145 pounds) and toughest eighth grader on the bus, Jack claimed the backseat for himself. His buddy Joey, as best friend to the toughest kid, was entitled to the other backseat.

I remember Jack proclaiming, "There is great honor in taking the backseat—but also great responsibility. From the backseat, I must make fart noises in my armpits, burp the 'Star-Spangled Banner,' and successfully sneak cell phones, iPods, and Game Boys onto the bus."

Diane and I were tolerant of Jack speaking like this, reasoning, as Diane often said, "It's good that Jack can speak honestly with his parents." So we looked the other way when Jack brought electronic devices onto the bus, even though we knew it was against school rules.

On a busy Monday, Diane called me at work to tell me that she'd been contacted by the assistant principal at Jack's school. She was on her way there. She didn't know the details, but said with angst, "It appears that Jack stole another boy's iPod. Matt, you should come."

"I have a huge proposal due on Wednesday. Will you please take care of this 'crisis' and tell me the results tonight?"

When I arrived home that evening, Jack was upstairs in his room. Diane burst out of the kitchen to report on the day's events.

"Jack took the iPod of a sixth grader on the bus this morning, and threatened to beat up the boy if he squealed. The boy nevertheless told the assistant principal, who pulled Jack out of class and searched his locker. Jack had accumulated three iPods, a cell phone, a cigarette lighter, and a *Hustler* magazine. Joey is in trouble too for his role in this mess." Diane went on, "Jack is suspended from school until he and Joey return the goods they have bullied away from other children. I'm beside myself with shame and disappointment," she said tearfully.

Diane's a good mother, with only two weaknesses: She's easily seduced by the newest shiny piece of crap placed on end-of-aisle displays at Target; and she's completely unable to muster any toughness in dealing with Jack, no matter how much it is warranted. The first weakness bothers me more often, but the second weakness is far more serious. It places me permanently in the "asshole" role when it is time to come down hard on Jack.

I trudged upstairs.

JACK'S ROOM at the time was quintessential young teenage boy. On the walls were posters of his favorite historical military machines—the B-29, the armored World War II bomber nicknamed the "Flying Fortress," and the ironclads, the *Monitor* and the *Merrimac,* in pitched battle. There were also posters of Jack's two favorite athletes: Peyton Manning, the prolific TV pitchman who continues to moonlight as quarterback for the Indianapolis

Colts, and Triple H, a mass of muscle who play-acts hitting people with a sledgehammer each week on WWE wrestling. Every inch of dresser top was filled with sports trophies fallen on top of each other. Since every boy and girl now gets a trophy for everything, trophies are just pieces of junk to my son's generation. Jack's burgeoning interest in girls had not yet progressed to pinups.

I came into his room and was met by that *Dad, let me explain, it's not as bad as it sounds* face. I started, "I heard some pretty amazing things about your conduct today, Jack. What do you want to tell me about it?" As the words came out, I realized that I had used this line or something like it to start three other conversations with him in the last two months.

Jack went into his explanation. "It started when Joey grabbed John Cermak's iPod and ran to the back of the bus with it. When Cermak came after Joey, I had to stick up for my friend. I shoved Cermak backwards and he backed away. From then on, Joey kept grabbing things and telling people I would beat up anyone who got in the way." This all sounded plausible—Joey was a very smart boy, but trouble. Jack was easily influenced for the worse by friends.

"Chip off the old block," I thought, as I listened.

I stated sternly, "Get together everything you have stolen and get in the car. And do it right now."

We returned all the stolen items that evening. As we drove from house to house, I lectured Jack about bullying. "Sure it hurts the victim, but it also coarsens the bully. Incidents like this will stay with you your entire life." Jack sat silently, presumably thinking his old man was either a big pussy or a Martian Overlord.

That night, Diane and I talked for an hour about how to punish Jack. We decided that because he had come clean and returned the goods, we'd let it go—but just this once.

JACK WAS never again involved in an extortion ring (at least to my knowledge), but there was a second incident on his middle school bus two months later. Again, Diane was contacted by the school, but this time she called me and said, "I don't have the strength to go again. Matt, you have to go."

After a long silence, I said "Fine."

Jack was again in cahoots with Joey and was again abusing other boys on the bus. The assistant principal told me, "It seems that Jack and Joey are forcing the other boys to come to the back of the bus to sing humiliating children's songs. Children who do not go willingly to the back of the bus, as warned by Joey, face Jack's so-called 'powers of persuasion.' At least five children went to the back of the bus and sang either, 'I'm a Little Teapot' or 'The Wheels on the Bus Go 'Round and 'Round.'"

On this last sentence, I choked down a laugh. I was glad the assistant principal didn't seem to notice. He went on, "Children who did not sing these songs with *feeling* and hand gestures were forced to sing the song again and again until their effort was judged satisfactory by Jack and Joey. Fortunately, all the selected children chose to sing in preference to being beaten up by Jack, so this sad joke did not result in any physical harm." I just barely maintained a concerned face through the entire melodramatic presentation.

Driving Jack home from school that day, I gruffly repeated the chorus of the song, "the wheels on the bus go 'round and 'round" as a way to voice my displeasure. But the anger left my voice as I pictured Jack holding court in the backseat of the bus and passing off pompous Simon Cowell-style critiques on each singer. Of course Jack's behavior was bad, but this was funny and no one was hurt. Besides, Jack was being a leader—the alpha male in the mini-*Lord of the Flies* drama of the school bus. I always wanted a son at the top of his peer pack. My voice lightened.

Jack pounced on the opening. "Hey Dad, you know what?"

"What Jack?"

"In addition to wheels on the bus going 'round and 'round, did you know that the wipers on the bus go swish, swish, swish?"

I laughed. I tried to stop, but couldn't. He sure is a pistol, I thought.

"Don't terrorize any more kids, or next time I will come down hard on you. Okay?"

Jack replied, "You betcha. Just call me Mother Teresa from this day forward."

In the three months following that statement, Mother Teresa was suspended from school for stealing a crate of chocolate milk, implicated (but not proven responsible) for the destruction of a string of mailboxes in our neighborhood, and caught smoking behind the bushes in back of our house. Jack deflected my attempts to engage him about all of this by either clamming up or wisecracking. When I reminded him that he was reneging on his "Mother Teresa" pledge, he replied, "The sainted mother was quite a hellion as a teen."

DISCUSSION WITH LISA:

Even before I sat down in the rocking chair, Lisa asked, "Is this story mostly about Jack, or you, or Diane?"

I settled in my chair. "That's a trick question. It's about all of the above. Shrink sessions are like the SATs, if you select 'D—All of the Above' you'll be correct most of the time."

She pushed on. "Cute, but what did you learn from this story? Let's take this one person at a time. Tell me about Jack when he was fourteen."

"Okay. I learned a few things. I learned that Jack was a bad kid in many ways, but mostly he was a weak kid. Not physically, of course, but mentally. He had no ability to assess right and wrong, and couldn't step away from a friend who was taking him in the wrong direction. Like his old man, he learned to use his sense of humor to dodge hard questions and deflect people away from uncomfortable topics—and Jack walked away from his own promise to behave. This set him up to do something far more damaging eighteen months later."

"What about Diane?"

"Diane is a loving mother and a kind person—but she's made out of tissue paper. She's inconsequential. She has no stomach for the tougher side of parenting, and leaves me to handle all the unpleasantness. It's not fair."

Lisa prodded, "And what else?"

I looked across to see Lisa staring at me as I squirmed in my chair. There was silence. Finally I said, "I must share my feelings with Diane. She must understand that I need her to step up when times are hard."

"And tell me what this story says about Matthew Duffy?"

"I failed my son. I was secretly pleased that he was becoming a bad-ass and I was half-hearted in steering him away from his bad behavior. Here and elsewhere, Jack needed a good kick in the head, not literally, of course. I mean that he needed a firm course correction. Like Diane, I didn't always have the stomach for being firm with him. I suppose I was no better than she was." I stopped and took a sip of water. The truth is supposed to be invigorating, but this truth made me a little sick.

"So, is this story mostly about Jack, you, or Diane?" Lisa repeated.

"I guess this story really is about all three of us."

Lisa nodded, "That's a positive outcome—even if your conclusions are disappointing."

But I was feeling no joy. "How do you see any positive outcomes here?"

"I understand that your conclusions are not happy ones. But you're now exploring interconnections in your stories. They are no longer just simple narrations about a particular person. You've come a long way."

I smiled. I don't know when it happened, but I really was using these stories to teach me about myself.

"Lisa, you know we've never discussed Jack's attempted suicide. It's all that's really left for us to talk about, isn't it?"

"I would not say it that way," Lisa replied, "but it probably is the biggest topic that we haven't covered."

"Okay, I'm going to tell you about it and the part I played. I haven't talked to anyone about why Jack slit his wrists—not McGowan, not Kevin, not Lynette, not my father. Diane and I don't even talk about it." I choked up a little.

Lisa's expression softened. "Over the last half-year, you've made big strides. Writing about this won't be easy, and you probably will not have a lovely epiphany as a result. But you have to deal with it and I think you're ready to try."

I nodded.

19

A Little Ditty 'bout Jack and Diane

Jill Silva was Jack's first little "girlfriend" and girls have been sweet on him ever since. Jack never thought twice about any of them—until he became friends with Diane Zabeen Hymes.

The Hymes family moved into East Princeton when Jack was fourteen. They bought a small house on the opposite side of our subdivision. Like Jack, Diane was an only child, atypical in East Princeton. The entire Hymes family was atypical for East Princeton. Diane's father, Gerald Hymes, was a former diplomat for the State Department. He retired from federal service to take a lobbyist job in Trenton, representing a consortium of Asian manufacturers. Due to her father's frequent change in duty stations, Diane had lived in five foreign countries by age thirteen—Italy, Turkey, Thailand, Argentina, and Bangladesh. Four days in Cancun passed for world travel in East Princeton.

Diane's mother, Zabeen Rashketemi, came from an elite Iranian family that fled Iran for Germany in 1979 when the Shah was toppled. She matured into a European sophisticate. But while briefly working for an international do-gooder group in Bangladesh, Zabeen had a fling with Hymes and became pregnant. Zabeen and Gerald discussed abortion as the preferred way out of their predicament, though the poor medical care available in Bangladesh (rightly) scared Zabeen. They selected the next best option—they married. Gerald was forty, Zabeen twenty-one. She was disowned by her family. Gerald was long estranged from his.

By age fifteen, Diane Zabeen Hymes was physically mature with curves in all the right places. She had her dad's delicate WASP blue eyes, and her mom's mocha complexion and full lips. Her wardrobe was sexy and sophisticated—dominated by bright satin tops from Italy and Turkey that were always a size too small. They revealed her flat midriff and exposed the tops of her breasts. She wore meticulously faded, torn jeans straight out of the wardrobe of Brittany Spears (before Ms. Spears became bald, tubby, and psychotic). Diane's hair was long, jet black, and chemically straightened. She tied it in a single ponytail, coquettishly pulled around the front so that it dangled just above her blouse-line, brushing against the tops of her breasts.

Jack and Diane became special friends. She was at our house most evenings when I came home from work, to say nothing of the weekends. I caught them kissing many times. I'd shout "break it up" and they would, at least until I left the room. I knew that Jack really liked her when he sat through *My Big Fat Greek Wedding* without complaining. No other person on the planet could have forced him to watch that movie.

Diane was at our house so often that I once jokingly suggested we call her "Young Diane" and my wife "Old Diane" to avoid confusion. Though I said this in jest, Jack and Joey seized upon the names and they stuck. My wife still winces every time the nickname is used—but for clarity, I will use these labels for the rest of this story.

———

As JACK'S best friend, Joey could have become a jerk when Jack started falling for Young Diane. But, as far as I can tell, Joey adjusted well. Of course, as a consummate wise-ass, Joey took his shots at Young Diane. I once overheard him call her "Helen Keller."

I asked Joey, "What's up with the nickname?"

"It's because, Mr. Duffy, those jeans are so tight I can read her lips. Uh, sorry Mr. Duffy, you never heard me say that, okay?"

I just smiled and turned away. The coarse joke didn't bother me. Joey took shots at everyone, and Young Diane seemed to like the recognition that her wardrobe was provocative.

Eye candy aside, I thought Young Diane was a nice girl and good for Jack. She'd bring little treats—like homemade baklava—to our house when she came over. I liked her parents. Gerald Hymes gave me his copies of fancy academic journals like *Current History* when he was done with them, and I enjoyed reading them on weekend afternoons. Since the Hymeses were estranged from their extended families, and I was largely estranged from mine, I invited them over for barbecues on lazy summer weekends. On those occasions, five out of six of us had a good time.

Old Diane was bothered by the young libertine, Zabeen Hymes. Diane's dislike of Mrs. Hymes was sealed at the Labor Day barbecue when the drunk Zabeen offered an R-rated family history culminating with a description of her daughter as "an unwanted child." Old Diane's jaw dropped.

Changing the subject, I noted, "The two kids have drifted off."

Zabeen started singing, to the tune of John Cougar Mellencamp's song, *Life Goes On,* "A little ditty about Jack and Diane, two American kids taking it in the can." Zabeen laughed at her cleverness.

When Old Diane looked disapproving, Zabeen offered, "Look, *Old Diane*, kids like to fool around. It is okay. *Young Diane* is on the pill."

Old Diane was mortified; she said, "I have a terrible headache," and went inside.

———

SHORTLY BEFORE Jack's relationship with Young Diane blossomed, Old Diane went back to work. Jack was a handful, but I rationalized, "Giving Jack some space might help him mature." But mostly, we needed to make up for lost time on Jack's college fund.

Although Jack was a poor student, we both expected him to attend college. Even with poor grades, there would be some mediocre college somewhere that would take him. I told Diane, "There are dozens of colleges that cater to the least able children of the most able parents."

Diane showed me a *Newsweek* article about colleges employing lower admission standards for applicants who forego financial aid. So the plan was to use Diane's income to bribe some down-on-its-luck college into accepting our underachieving son. I straightened out in college; Jack would too.

After fifteen years as a stay-at-home mom, Diane was hired as the kindergarten teacher at a small evangelical school in Flemington. She was offered the job only after lying about "the commanding role of Jesus Christ" in her life.

Diane made it home from teaching by four-fifteen. Jack's school let out at three-thirty, and the buses dropped off the teens by three-fifty. Within minutes, Young Diane rode her bike to our house. Old Diane complained, "I don't like seeing Diane Zabeen's bicycle in the driveway every day when I come home. It means Jack is alone in the house with that girl." Because of this, Old Diane reversed her position on Jack's friendship with Joey. She started calling him a "firecracker" instead of a "troublemaker." Now, Old Diane encouraged Joey to come over. She stocked the pantry with pizza-flavored Combos (Joey's favorite snack food) even though no one in our family ate them. Our family of three blossomed to a family of five. This was because, for Old Diane, a family of four was unacceptable.

Young Diane elevated Joey's wit. She introduced him to *The Onion* and his comic material went from Howard Stern-vulgar to Bill Maher-smug. Once, while driving Jack, Old Diane, Young Diane, and Joey to the beach, Joey started doing a gag in which he claimed to be "the Supreme Spokesperson for the North Korean

Ministry of Truth." In a rotten Korean accent, Joey noted, "It is with immense pride that I report to my American rivals that bellicose rhetoric has now surpassed misery as my country's number one export." As we passed Burger King, he further noted:

Ahh . . . You Americans enjoy our North Korean invention, the aggregated beef patty on milled grain. Of course, in North Korea we add dirt and the ground organs of South Korean fishermen to our aggregated beef patties. This makes our patties 1,000 times more delicious than yours. I see that some copycat American capitalist has parodied the name of our famous Northern Korean restaurant, Burger Kim. This causes your country great shame.

Jack, Young Diane, and I howled at Joey's political humor; Old Diane sat silent.

Besides political humor, Young Diane's influence on Jack and Joey was most apparent in their appearance. Prior to Young Diane's relationship with Jack, the two boys showed no interest in fashion. Jack never expressed any interest in clothing other than praising the occasional new sports jersey as "cool."

Young Diane changed that. Jack started wearing only black: black sleeveless T-shirts, black hooded sweatshirts, black synthetic pants, black socks, black boots, and black-mirrored sunglasses. I don't know where all the new clothes came from. I suspected shoplifting, but had no evidence. Jack's short hair grew longer— and was carefully combed by Young Diane each day after school to appear uncombed. More disturbing, Young Diane started cutting the boys on the arms as some kind of odd fashion statement. The cuts freaked out Old Diane; I agreed to investigate.

One afternoon I asked Jack, Joey, and Young Diane, "What's up with the fashion-noir?"

"We call it goth, Dad." Jack replied, as if I had been living on the moon for decades. He then mumbled something that I only half-understood about "the Trench Coat Mafia's New Jersey chapter."[1]

---

1. The Trench Coat Mafia was the name taken by the teen murderers who shot up their peers at Columbine High School in Colorado.

Young Diane quickly steered the conversation to safer territory. "We just love the look of the characters in the Matrix movies." But Young Diane was wearing a halter top that was a swirl of neon oranges and yellows. It seems she had a waiver on the all-black attire rule.

Young Diane and Jack spent hours together in his room. The door was always open because a rule of the house was "no female guests behind closed doors." But there were long stretches in which Old Diane or I were downstairs or even out of the house. Exactly what they did to fill all the time in Jack's room remains largely a mystery to me, but here is what I do know.

Jack's taste in video games moved toward grotesque. No longer content with the standard shoot-'em-up games from the local GameStop store, Jack and Young Diane explored the Internet in search of more shocking fare. They became fond of *So You Think You Can Drive, Mel?* in which the player is a drunk-driving Mel Gibson attempting to run down Jewish pedestrians. They also found a game called *Bllz: The League*, a football-gone-gladiator game where players pump themselves with steroids to become freakish beasts, and then maim opponents as a precursor to advancing the football. Initially, I found these games funny, and I even played them with Jack. I named my own muscle-freak "Hockey Rocky" and pumped him full of steroids.

Young Diane and Jack experimented with drugs and booze. I made a big ceremony out of pouring out a six-pack of Bud Lite that I found in the bushes in front of Jack, but I knew that more bottles were being consumed by the teens than confiscated by the parents. More troubling, the containers of Old Diane's prescription sleep aids and painkillers had mysteriously emptied. Since Jack knew that I pushed the envelope on drugs and booze as a teen, I had limited leverage on this topic. When Old Diane confronted Jack, he drowned her out by saying loudly, "blah-blah-blah" and walking away, leaving her teary and speechless.

The one time Old Diane and I pressed Jack about stealing Old Diane's prescription drugs, he smirked and replied, "I don't know much about Mom's drugs, other than the new one—I think it's called Darndiphino."

I got the joke (Darn'd-if-I-Know) and started laughing. When Old Diane did not get the joke even after Jack repeated the fictitious drug name several times—we both laughed. Old Diane left the room in disgust.

Jack later admitted that Young Diane had made up the name; they shouted "Darndiphino" when popping drugs without reading the container labels.

———

ONE SUMMER Sunday, Jack sat down next to me while I was reading on the patio. "Dad, do you love Mom?"

I heard myself answer, "Of course, we've been married for seventeen years." (Actually, it was eighteen.)

Jack gave me a look that suggested my quick answer was unsatisfactory. He tried again, "Okay Dad, let me say it this way. Are you *in-love* with Mom?"

This was a hard question. Of course I loved Diane, but after twenty years, life takes its toll on being *in-love*. I thought about the contentious parenting decisions, the hard choices we were making for Jack's college fund, the annual squawk about visiting Diane's obnoxious sister in Maryland, the stupid fight over the right shade of yellow paint for the kitchen, and the smoldering non-confrontations when a certain love-of-my-life keeps bringing home whatever the fuck she wants after we have previously agreed upon Chipotle. Of course, I was no longer *in-love* with Diane. Of course, I couldn't tell that to Jack.

I came up with what I thought was a pretty good answer. "*In-love* is a tough term, Jack. But if you mean, do your mother and I have the kind of passionate puppy love that young people experience when they are first dating, I think the answer is no. But I would contend we have something better, certainly more stable."

After a short pause Jack offered, "Well, I am *in love* with Diane, I mean Young Diane, of course. I want to spend my life with her. I want to marry her."

I tried to stay calm. "Ouch, Jack. You're still a kid. You don't even shave; you can't even manage a C in Math for the Nearly Retarded. I have no beef with your girlfriend. Heck, I like her too. But no more talk about marriage until your brain gets some control over your dick. Don't be a butt."

Jack looked at me with real disappointment, as if he thought there was a chance that I could be supportive of his declaration. As he picked himself up out of the lawn chair, I added, "If you know what's good for you, don't mention your feelings about Young Diane to Old Diane. It'll be the crisis of the century."

JACK WAS especially sullen and withdrawn that week. He left any room I entered. Old Diane cornered me one evening after Jack went to his room straight after dinner. She asked, "What the heck is going on between you two?"

Against my best instincts, I told her. "Jack told me he wants to marry Young Diane. I told him it wasn't a good idea. Now he hates me. Don't get hysterical about this."

In our twenty years together, I have coached Old Diane "not to get hysterical" maybe five times; it has never worked. We argued through the evening about various things: Jack's relationship with Young Diane, Jack's relationship with me, Jack's relationship with Old Diane, and, finally, my relationship with Old Diane.

When that was done, and when Old Diane had plowed through a box of tissues, I took a pillow and went downstairs to watch television. It was one AM. The light was still on in Jack's room. As I passed, Jack's door opened and he gave me a mocking thumbs-up sign. He said, "Way to go, Dad. I heard the whole thing."

I said, "You're a butt. Go to bed," and shut his door.

At work the next day, Old Diane called to tell me that she was booking us a hotel room in Philly for the coming Friday night.

We could use the time to discuss any lingering issues, but mostly she just wanted us to have a nice night together. I winced at the thought of canceling my scheduled beer with McGowan, but I didn't dare mention it. "That sounds lovely, Diane. I'll try to get out of the office a little early on Friday."

I HAD a hard time getting out of work that Friday, and didn't get home until six-thirty, my usual time. Graciously, Diane let my broken promise pass without comment. I gave Jack a few instructions that were received with only one-word responses: "fine," "understood," "nope." I reminded him about the rules of the house when we're away, i.e., no male guests past eleven, no female guests at all. Old Diane gave him a big hug. We were out of the house by six forty-five.

Traffic on the New Jersey Turnpike was horrendous. It's always bad on summer Fridays. Everyone in New York empties out of the Empire State using the turnpike as their route to anywhere else. The New Yorkers pile atop masses of New Jerseyians on their way to backyard barbecues a few exits to the north or south. Diane and I got on the turnpike at Exit 7A at seven and didn't reach Exit 7, only five miles away, until seven-thirty. Neither Diane nor I had eaten—we were starving.

She said, "Let's change plans and stay local." I nodded yes. Diane called the hotel in Philly and canceled our reservation. We turned around and went to one of the new bistros in Princeton. School was out, so getting a table was not a problem.

The revised plan went without a hitch. By eight, we were sitting at a corner table at Za, a lovely Italian bistro on the outskirts of the village. Two bottles of wine over dinner lubricated the conversation, and made me funny. Between courses, I reached out and held her hand. She cooed like a dove. Diane drove us home because I was drunk. It was about eleven PM.

The house was dark as we pulled into the driveway. As the garage door started rising, a light came on in Jack's room. I told

Diane, "Stop the car and watch the front door." Diane said, "Sure, but what . . . ?"

I was out of the car before she could finish her question. I ran around to the back of the house and stood outside the back door, rocking on the balls of my feet. Twenty seconds later, the back door flew open, Jack and Young Diane came running out half-naked, expecting to successfully make a break for it. I blocked their escape.

I was full of myself for catching them red-handed and bare-chested. I grabbed the bundle of clothes out of Jack's hand. "Jack, your loose friend needs to go home. I guess she can do this after she gets dressed." Jack waited as Young Diane put on her bra and shirt in front of me; I was too drunk to realize the complete inappropriateness of the moment.

My finger caught upon something rough and metallic in the bundle of clothes. I pulled it out. Squinting, I held it up to the glint of light coming through the back window of the garage. It was a ring—it was an engagement ring.

I said, "Oh shit, no." Then I ran into our little backyard, and threw the ring into the woods beyond our backyard fence. Jack ran into the house, upstairs to his room, and locked his door. Old Diane drove the now-clothed Young Diane home.

———

OLD DIANE nodded off about one AM. I nodded off a little after that, but was too wound up to fall into a deep sleep. About three-fifteen, I heard footsteps on the stairs and then I heard the door to Jack's room close. About three-thirty I heard Jack's muffled voice groan, "Ahhh . . . unn . . . ya-yee."

Now wide awake, I sat up listening for more sounds but heard none. After a few minutes, I decided I would look in on Jack. I went to open his door, but it was locked. I called his name several times quietly, but there was no response. I called his name loudly—still no response. I shivered as a terrible thought ran through my mind.

"Jack, open the door now!" I said loudly and sternly. No response!

"Open the fucking door now, you little shit. I mean it!" I yelled. No response!!

I heard Diane groggily ask, "Is anything wrong?" I ignored her and put my shoulder hard into the door. The builder's-grade door split easily as I stumbled into the room.

My boy had slit his wrist wide open on his left arm, and slightly on his right. Two pools of blood were beside each arm and he was unconscious. There was blood all over, including up and down the blade of the carving knife he'd taken from the kitchen. The blood had thoroughly soaked into his sheets and was dripping onto the carpet. I noticed Diane's bottles of Darndiphino next to Jack on his bed. They were all empty.

"Jesus!—Jack? Jack? Jack." I said as I hugged him gently. "Diane, call 911."

Jack lost three quarts of blood, but it could have been much worse. The paramedics praised me for applying direct pressure to his wounds during the twenty minutes before they arrived. They told me that it probably saved his life. Jack was admitted to Princeton Hospital for an attempted suicide at four-forty AM, July 20, 2009.

He had composed a brief suicide note to his girlfriend.

> Diane,
>
> I am sorry to do this to you. I am in love with you, but you can do better than me. As my father and everyone else keep telling me, I am a butt.
>
> Find someone else.
>
> Jack

PHYSICALLY, JACK recovered quickly, and he was discharged from the hospital after only two days. During those two days Diane and

I met with a police officer who specializes in suicides, and then we met with the same police officer and Mercer County social services. The next day there was a third meeting, with all the same people plus Jack's high school principal and guidance counselor. My dominant recollection from that meeting was the police officer dozing off as the social workers and school officials played *Can you top this?* with increasingly imbecilic coping-with-suicide suggestions.

Diane found three books about dealing with suicidal people and read each book cover to cover. She attempted to implement every single suggestion in each of them. It took every ounce of restraint I could muster not to wisecrack. But there were some very helpful suggestions that I embraced wholeheartedly, including the development of a "safety plan" for Jack, which we put into effect. This included:

- Performing a "top to bottom" inspection of the house resulting in the confiscation of numerous dangerous items and placing our knives and household poisons in locked cabinets.
- Selecting a therapist to meet with Jack once a week. We interviewed three shrinks, and allowed Jack to make the final selection.
- Printing laminated cards of "helpful contacts" including social services, Jack's therapist, the family doctor, and a suicide prevention hotline. We all carry these cards in our wallets now, and cards are kept in strategic places throughout the house.
- Pulling Jack out of all violent activities, including karate and wrestling. We enrolled him in tennis lessons and the Boy Scouts. The scoutmasters keep a special eye on Jack and he's excelled as a scout.
- After three months of seeing different doctors, getting referrals, and lobbying my insurance company for coverage, I started seeing a shrink. An unintended consequence of which is this book.

After much discussion, Diane and I decided not to tell our families about Jack's near-suicide. For Diane, this decision was motivated by shame. I was motivated by a belief that the conversation with Dad would be a pain in the ass.

———

THE WEEKS following the attempted suicide went okay. Joey turned out to be a great friend to Jack—I never thought he had it in him. Two or three times a week, he stopped by to say hello and hang out. Each Friday night, he came over with a movie that his generation considers "classic." These have included *A Fish Called Wanda* (1988) and *Cape Fear* (1991), movies that I had considered "recent." Before bringing over *Cape Fear*, Joey sent me an email to make sure that the violent scenes in the movie "would be acceptable" to me and "not dangerous for Jack."

I was touched by Joey's consideration and told him so when he showed up. The boys now stay in on Friday nights, make themselves popcorn, and watch Joey's movie of the week. I spontaneously hugged Joey on one of those nights and didn't immediately let go when he pushed off. Joey cracked, "Thanks for the hug, Mr. Duffy, but I am not that kind of boy. I think you might have better luck at Holy Name."

As for Young Diane and Jack, that is more complicated. She and Jack still email frequently, and go to the movies together, chaperoned by Zabeen Hymes. But Young Diane has ratcheted-down their relationship and they are no longer intimate. I think she still likes him, but I imagine she now sees him as dangerously unstable. I suppose she's right in this regard.

Zabeen told Young Diane, "You must put some distance between you and Jack." Zabeen Hymes told me this offhandedly one afternoon when we bumped into each other at the 7-Eleven. The cooling-off saddened Jack for awhile, but only for awhile.

Two months ago, Jack met a girl at tennis lessons—Leslie something. She fancies him. I don't think he likes her that much, but they go out regularly. Mostly, I think he's pleased that a pretty, athletic girl likes him. Diane and I don't hear him talk about Young Diane anymore.

THE FINAL DISCUSSION WITH LISA:

It took me three weeks to write this story. During that time, I skipped two appointments. When I finally sent the story to Lisa it was poorly proofed and disorganized. It was the only time I sent her a story in bad shape.

As I entered Lisa's office that day, I asked, "What do you think?"

"I think you've been playing hooky because this was a hard story for you to write—and from a literary perspective, it is your worst product." Then she shrugged and smiled a little, "Hey, no worries."

Her smile made all the difference. "Guilty as charged," I said as I slid into my rocking chair.

Lisa came prepared with several questions, and didn't wait. "Do you think the romance with Diane Hymes was a major factor in your son's attempted suicide?"

"Thanks for starting with a softball. Yes. He fell for her in a very dangerous way. This was more than a regular teen crush."

"Why did Diane Hymes have such a tremendous influence over your son?"

"'Why' questions are always the most difficult. Diane Hymes was, I mean is, smart, hot and exotic. This is a powerful combo for a boy with an under-stimulated mind. If Francine Miglino gave me the time of day when I was a teen, I could have fallen for her just as hard." I sighed, "Diane's love for Jack, Old Diane that is, was smothering and trite; mine was socked away in a vault. Jack needed someone to care about him in a more meaningful way."

"Why did you attempt to deal with the dangerous parts of your son's romance without your wife's partnership?"

My first impulse was to respond defensively, or to say something insulting. But I tamed these worst instincts and said, "Ouch, baby!" in an Austin Powers voice.

I moved on. "My wife has a track record of going AWOL during the tough moments. If I am having problems with Jack, Diane only complicates things. But my curtness led Jack to clam up. His mother would have drawn him out, even if driving both of us crazy. I made a mistake. I won't make the same mistake again."

"Why did you tell me that you saved your son's life by applying direct pressure to his wounds?"

"Because it's true," I responded defensively. Then I remembered previous discussions and Lisa's statements about cherry-picking facts to create the narrative I want. "Well, that's not the entire story. I included this fact because I wanted to tell you—no, I needed to tell myself—that I saved my son's life. I needed a measure of redemption in the story."

"How's Jack doing now? Might he try to commit suicide again?"

Rocking in my chair, "Jack's doing better, generally. He still bullies weaker children sometimes and this troubles me, but he hasn't been in a single fight since the attempted suicide. He's befriended Russell Ridley, the autistic boy in our neighborhood, and is doing great in the Boy Scouts. I know that once suicidal, a person may try again, but I'm optimistic. Jack will turn out okay."

As I finished, I knew I had given Lisa the answers she wanted to hear. More important, I knew I had successfully confronted the most difficult moment in my life. I smiled. I was proud of myself.

I could not tell for sure, but I think Lisa's eyes were a little puffy. I think I heard some tightness in her throat. "From what you've told me, I think Jack is on a better path and I think you are on a trajectory to be a good parent to him."

"I really, really hope that is true." I said softly.

———

LISA AND I continued to meet for another two months after this final story. But the sessions devolved into me offering offhanded opinions on bullying, adolescence, and pop culture. I reported each week about the progress I was making in turning my stories into a real book. Finally, Lisa said, "Matthew, I think we're done."

At our last session, she had praised me. "You're a quick learner and a good writer. I wish you luck with your son, your marriage, and your book. Keep writing—it's good for you."

As I left her office for the last time, I asked if I could include excerpts of our shrink sessions in the book. She said, "Yes, but I would like to see the manuscript before it goes out to any publisher."

I emailed it to her a month later, and we met for lunch to discuss it. After pointing out a few small editorial gaffes and errors of fact, Lisa stopped herself. "This is minor stuff. All of my editorial comments are penciled on the manuscript, and you can take that with you. I think your book is very good. It is sad and honest and funny. Congratulations."

We talked about different parts of the book. Lisa was a great sport about my characterizations of her as George Washington on Mt. Rushmore, and we laughed about a few of my unsuccessful attempts to unnerve and sidetrack her with my wisecracks. Then we talked about the Dog, no longer as a ghost haunting me, but now as a literary character. I asked, "Do you think anyone will believe he was a real person?"

We talked about the ideas I had for a book title, and I confessed to not liking any of them very much. Then she put down her napkin and looked at me, "I think you should title the book, *A Thinking Man's Bully*."

"That's perfect." I stuck out my hand to high-five her; she reached across the table and whacked it.

Finally, I gave Lisa a folder with a "final" story that I wrote after our last session. I walked around the restaurant parking lot for twenty minutes as she read it. When I sat back down, Lisa pronounced: "This is a fitting end to your book, Matthew, and proof that you can get yourself to the right place."

20

The Redeeming Power of
Beavis and Butt-Head

Jack just turned sixteen. He's two inches taller than me and his broad shoulders suggest that he'll soon fill out at 200 pounds. The scars on his wrists are fading from red to fleshy pink. He favors long sleeve surfer pullovers to hide them. He's grown his hair so long that it touches his shoulders. While his surfer-dude appearance is out of place in suburban New Jersey, he is a good-looking boy. He is fortunate to have his mother's warm smile, thin nose, and athletic body. He has inherited almost nothing from me, except a mean sense of humor and an inability to focus in school.

Jack is a Boy Scout going for Eagle Scout. In uniform, he's a model citizen. All adults are addressed as Mr. or Ms. and he happily participates in many do-gooder activities. Outside of structured activities, however, he's still a wreck. The fresh egg stains on the Banjari house up the street are the most recent evidence of his continued bad behavior. He continues to push around the two freshmen at his bus stop.

Diane and I keep Jack engaged in after-school activities to minimize the unstructured time. I lecture Jack frequently about the bullying. He endures it, and, when given an opportunity, counter-punches at me for my hypocrisies.

A few weekends ago, I was driving Jack home from a camping weekend with the Boy Scouts in the mountains. We are usually cautious in our conversations with each other to avoid giving the other ammunition that can be used later. But this was a long drive and our defenses came down. Jack started telling me about the hike to a fire tower the previous day. Throughout the hike, the boys spoke in the over-the-top Aussie accents of Steve Irwin, the recently deceased star of *Crocodile Hunter*, and the improbably named Bear Grylles, who hosts *Man vs. Wild* on the Discovery Channel.

Jack joked with his friends about "urinating into my Nalgene for essential hydration during the torturous trek." He also joked about "rounding up the indigenous Mountain People for display in suburban zoos." Slipping into his own faux-Aussie accent, Jack described the pens in which the "indigenes would be placed for the delight of the college-educated and their progeny." Jack described a pen in which "a dozen half-starved mountain people 'rassle within an inch of expiration for a single can of SPAM," and a second pen in which "a sadistic dentist sets about the grimly satisfying task of filling in the hundred-plus cavities strewn across the mouths of six or seven mountain people."

Though the humor was coarse and condescending, I laughed with Jack through his stories. They were the big tear-inducing, stress-relieving laughs that come only once every few years. He told me about favorite lines and plot twists from different *South Park* episodes that inspire his sense of humor. Then I entertained him with the best lines and plots from *Beavis and Butt-Head* episodes that he was too young to know.

Jack made me promise that we'd get a *Beavis and Butt-Head* DVD and watch it together the next time Diane went shopping. Then we laughed again about his mother's dippy materialism and the digs we both take at her.

I started telling some of my old high school stories, including my abuse of Mr. Salty and Hockey Rocky, McGowan's annihilation of the three preppies, Uncle Kevin's homophobic rage, and my high school romance with Jeannie Small. Jack laughed hard during each story. Some were the knowing laughs shared between members of the fraternity of past and present bullies; other laughs were at my expense for being such a dork at his age. He summed things up, "Ouch, Dad, you were a bully *and* a dork. Not many kids are both a hammer and a nail. Usually it's one or the other." I agreed but told him, "I'm still haunted about being a hammer, not about being a nail."

Then Jack started telling a story from his childhood. "Dad, do you remember going crazy when I was eight? You called me a shithead and hit me so hard I had a huge bruise on my back. This was after I put my pet frogs, Battle Tank and Sniper Gun, on top of your high school yearbook. I guess this left a few pages soaked and dirty."

My anger rose at the charge, and I told him, "You are totally out of line. I did nothing more than give you a spank on the butt." I then heard this lunatic shout at Jack, "And what kind of rotten son gets a woody from accusing his father of child abuse? Who's the suicidal derelict in this car, anyway?"

Jack flushed red, and fired back, "Well, your bullying stories are as bad as anything as I have done—probably worse. Let's ask Mr. Salty or Hockey Rocky about what a great guy you were as a teenager. I think your pot-smoking has left you with a selective memory." I was stung by the strong comeback and ashamed. I muttered some profanities under my breath.

Jack looked at me and clinched the conversation, "Dude, truth hurts, but don't go Unabomber on me."

The next hour in the car was quiet. Again and again, I ran through Jack's version of the yearbook incident and the alleged child abuse. Each time I was able to remember the event a little more clearly, and strip away a little more of the post-event spin. It strained my mind to do this. At first I remembered nothing more than a well-measured spank to the ass and was sure that was correct. Then I remembered grabbing Jack hard by the arm; I remembered his squealing as I wrenched him away from the yearbook. I remembered my hand coming down hard with a slap against his ass and then a second time with, forgive me God, a fist in the small of his back. He cried and I made fun of him for crying by squishing up my face, putting it an inch from his, and loudly mocking him with exaggerated whimpers. Then I said something like, "Stand in the closet, because I can't stand looking at my shithead son. And if you ever tell your mother about this, we'll do this again, only next time I'll be *really* angry."

When the whole memory reemerged, I started sweating. I felt nauseous. I looked at Jack, who was sitting with his head turned away from me, but I had nothing so say.

As I pulled the car onto our street, I knew I had to come clean. I tried to speak, but couldn't push out any words. Finally, I found some, albeit stiff ones: "Jack, I admit that your account of the yearbook incident is more correct than mine. I am sorry— sorrier than you'll ever know. And if there were other times that I behaved this way, I apologize for those too. You are my son, and I love you."

There was no response. I turned into the driveway.

As I placed the car in park, I looked over and we made eye contact. Jack's eyes were puffy, his cheeks flushed. There was another half-minute of silence. He cracked a smile, "Thanks for apologizing, Dad. I know it makes you crazy when I pick on other kids, and I will really try to stop it—even when the dorks deserve it. Just kidding. Hey, get me that *Beavis and Butt-Head* DVD and we'll call it a down payment on my future good behavior."

He then pulled his shirt over his head, and exclaimed, "I am Corn-holio. I need tee-pee for my bung hole!" in an imitation of my imitation of the drug-tripping Beavis. We exchanged additional *Beavis and Butt-Head* lines as we exited the car.

I entered the house and kissed Diane. I looked at her, "I know I am a hard person to love. Thank you for still loving me." She smiled and teared up.

I went upstairs and dialed my father. When he answered, I didn't pause. "Dad, a year ago Jack attempted suicide and nearly killed himself. We hooked him up with some good professionals, and he's doing much better now. I was seeing a shrink until a few weeks ago. I'm doing better too."

"Oh, shit. A year ago? Thank God Jack's okay. How are you doing?" Dad's voice became soft and weak. "Why didn't you tell me until now? Why didn't you want my help?"

"Dad, I'm writing a book about all of this. I want you to read it."